HOW TO STEAL A GOD'S HEART

LESSONS IN DIVINE DISASTERS

CARRIE PULKINEN

How to Steal a God's Heart

ISBN: 978-1-957253-47-3

previously published as Sign Steal Deliver

CHAPTER ONE

"Now this is what I call a party." Hermes rolled his Ducati to a stop at the corner of Dumaine and Bourbon Street as a mass of humans dressed in togas and laurels danced down the center of the road. A five-piece brass band belted out a lively tune as they hung a right at the intersection and continued on their way, and Hermes tapped his foot on the pavement along with the beat.

He held up his wrist so Agnes and Avernus, the snakes spiraling up his caduceus, could see the revelry. Carrying a full-length staff around in public made it difficult to keep his identity a secret—which old Z insisted all the Olympians do—so he shrank it to wristwatch size and wore it as a bracelet most of the time. "What do you think? Best vacation ever?"

"It isss an interesting placccceee," Agnes hissed.

"But would they sssstill be honoring you if they knew you were retired?" Avernus asked.

"It's a good thing they don't know. Isn't it, Vern?" Hermes winked, and the wings on his helmet fluttered in excitement as he continued his trip to Esplanade toward the vacation rental he'd booked on FaeBNB.

It wasn't difficult to convince the rest of the Olympians their next road trip should be to New Orleans. With parade organizations—AKA krewes—named specifically for the gods, how could they say no to a two-week-long party thrown in their honor?

Sure, Z was a little ticked to find out there was a Krewe of Poseidon but no Krewe of Zeus. It didn't help when he learned some minor gods like Iris, Morpheus, and even the hero Perseus had parades but the king of the gods got nada. Hell, Dionysus got two: one for his Greek name and one for his Roman, Bacchus.

Hermes had tried to explain the streets weren't wide enough for all that ego, but when dear old dad was about to put his foot down on the whole trip, Hermes changed his tune. He convinced Z the entire carnival honored the king of the gods and the mortals would have warred over who got to be in the Krewe of Zeus. Z bought it, of course.

Hey, Hermes was good with words. He was the god of language, after all.

With Poseidon, Dionysus, Athena, and finally Zeus on board, the others had no choice but to follow. So, they all hopped on their bikes—well, all but Hera, who towed her bike behind the SUV so her helmet wouldn't mess up her hair—and made the three-day trip from Seattle to New Orleans.

Three days to travel 2,600 miles. Can you imagine? Hermes could have made the trip in twelve hours, keeping his wheels on the pavement the entire way. But the god of speed had to slow it down and ride with the pack at a tortoise's pace…and everyone knew tortoises were better off as lyres. Just ask Apollo.

After parking in the driveway, Hermes slipped off his helmet and gazed at the two-story white mansion with green shutters that would be their home for the next few weeks. His wings fluttered again, always anxious to hit the road, and he stroked the golden feathers, smoothing them back against his helmet. "Calm down, boys; we're staying put for a while."

The wings quivered in protest, but the snakes hissed their approval. "Finally," Agnes said. "I was getting motion sssick."

Hermes slid off the bike and took his suitcase from the side pannier. There was no way in Hades his bike could hold two weeks' worth of clothes, much less shoes and accessories, even with the special touring package. Lucky for Hermes, and all the gods, Z let them keep their magical powers along with their immortality when they shut down Olympus so enchanting the side panniers to hold as much as he needed was a no-brainer. He couldn't depend on Hera to carry all his stuff in the SUV. Who knew how long it would take her to get here? Besides, he was the cleverest of all the gods. He helped them, not the other way around.

He walked up the porch steps and found the keys and paperwork in a basket by the front door, just where the landlord said they would be. The house sat in the perfect location, a block away from the French Quarter, but far enough from all the action that they could have some privacy when they wanted it.

Inside, Hermes' riding boots thudded on the hardwood floor as he made his way through the foyer. A spacious living area sat to the right, with a maroon sofa and loveseat and six cream-colored chairs positioned around a massive fireplace. Light that baby up, and Hades would feel right at home. To the left stood the dining room, complete with an oblong table with seating for sixteen.

He scoped out the bedrooms, passing up the master because Z would throw a fit if Hermes claimed that one. At the top of the stairs, the first room on the right had pale pink carpet, pink curtains, and, hell… everything in there was pink. It was like fifty shades of Pepto Bismol. Perfect for Hera.

The room for Hermes sat at the end of the long hallway. It was decorated in muted earth tones, and the *pièce de résistance* was the small balcony overlooking the back courtyard. As the god of travel, Hermes couldn't stand being cooped up inside for long. This would be his place of escape when he needed a rest from the revelry.

The sound of boots thudding on the porch and deep ricochets of laughter resonated through the house as Hermes set his suitcase on the dresser. The rest of the gods had finally arrived.

"Took you long enough." He grinned as he descended the staircase and tossed each Olympian a house key.

Athena scoffed, brushing her dark hair behind her shoulders. "If you hadn't left us in the dust the moment we hit I-10, we'd have arrived at the same time."

"I couldn't help myself. All that open road with the swamp on either side…" He sighed wistfully. "What can I say? I have a need for speed."

And a need to occasionally put some distance between himself and the other gods and their massive egos. They rode like they owned the road, expecting everyone else to yield to them even when they didn't have the right of way. The gods might have ruled on Mount Olympus, but now that they lived on Earth—and were supposedly not meddling in mortal affairs—they really needed to let go of their hyped-up self-worth.

"I have a need to get out of these riding clothes and slip into something more seductive," Aphrodite purred.

"Bedrooms are on the second floor." Hermes gestured to the staircase. "I claimed the master since I got here first."

Z's brow slammed down over his eyes. "It's bad enough you get a parade and I don't. You're not getting the master bedroom too."

Hermes laughed. "I'm kidding, old man. The big guy gets the big room. I know the rules." Though he'd be the first to break them. Any. Chance. He. Got. And why not? He was a glorified errand boy in their eyes. He'd spent his entire existence accommodating them, helping them out when they got into sticky situations, *stealing* for them when they wanted something they weren't supposed to have. And how did they repay him? By expecting him to do more, that was how.

Since they wanted to treat him like a joke, that was exactly what he'd given them, becoming a trickster, playing pranks and using his cunning and wit instead of flexing like a...well, like a self-important god.

"Hey, Hermes." Hades shoved a manila envelope toward him. "I need you to take this down to Medusa in the underworld. It's got to be there this afternoon."

See what I mean? Hermes held up his hands, refusing to take it. "I'm not your messenger boy anymore, man. I'm retired, just like the rest of you." Why did they have such a hard time accepting that?

"Someone's got to pay Medusa's salary," Hades huffed, narrowing his eyes. "When she agreed to stay in the underworld, it wasn't from the kindness of her stone-cold heart. She's doing it to get paid. I'm already two days late sending her check, thanks to your vacation plans, and if she doesn't get it soon, she'll quit. Do you really want all those souls finding their way to the earthly realm?"

Hermes rolled his eyes and tugged his phone from

his pocket. His brooding uncle could be so dramatic, and while Hermes really was done running errands for them, he couldn't resist helping him out. *Old habits die hard.* A five-second search provided what he needed, so he texted the website to Hades. "Problem solved."

"What's this?" Hades squinted at his phone. "What's a nog?"

"N-O-G-S. New Orleans Ghostal Service." Hermes scanned the website. "Need something delivered fast? We'll spirit it away in no time. Satisfaction guaranteed."

Hades pursed his lips, nodding. "That could work. Thanks." At least he offered a little gratitude this time.

As the gods got settled into their rooms, Hermes changed into dark brown slacks and a buttercream button-up. Winged cufflinks completed the ensemble, and he strolled onto the front porch, sinking into a wicker chair while he waited for Athena's battle plan. The goddess of war and wisdom had an itinerary scheduled for every damned day of Mardi Gras, and Hermes would humor her and follow it for the time being.

Near the house next door, a group of college-age boys—mere children to a thousands-year-old god—

stood on the sidewalk, drinking green liquid from plastic yard glasses. Strands of colorful beads encircled their necks, and many were shirtless beneath, reminding him of Dion in his younger years.

Dionysus was the first god to jump onboard when Hermes suggested this trip, and he could see why. The god of wine and festivity would feel right at home in a place like this.

Hermes leaned back in his chair, lacing his fingers behind his head and extending his legs as he soaked in the scene. Enormous oak trees dotted the median—or neutral ground in the local dialect—and two- and three-story houses lined the thoroughfare, their façades painted in muted shades of yellow, white, and brown.

The college boys whistled as a woman riding a powder-blue Vespa rounded the corner. She parked on the curb in front of the guys and slid off the scooter before stepping onto the sidewalk and turning toward Hermes.

Her long, dark brown hair was swept back behind her shoulders, and a light coat of shimmery pink eye shadow accented her brown eyes and olive skin perfectly. She wore brown pants with a purple short-sleeved button-up that had the acronym NOGS embroidered on the breast.

Hermes' breath caught, and his pulse kicked up as she checked something on her phone. As the messenger god, he held an affinity for those in the courier business, and as a hot-blooded man, he couldn't deny her beauty. Though mortals rarely ever prayed to the Olympians for assistance these days, he'd be happy to bless this delivery woman with a little extra speed and safety on her journey.

As she slipped her phone into her back pocket and strode toward the gods' rental home, one of the college kids caught her by the wrist. "Where you going, sweetheart?" he drawled.

Hermes leaned forward in his chair as a strange urge to protect this woman he'd never met overcame him. Well, maybe it wasn't completely strange. She was a courier, one of his people, but this urge felt stronger than anything he could recall.

"Hmm…" A slow smile curved the woman's lips, and she placed her free hand on the boy's shoulder. "I'm going to pick up a delivery. Where are you going?" Her voice was seductive, a purr that could give Aphrodite a run for her money.

The guy let out a cocky laugh and released her arm, which she immediately slid behind his back. "How about you forget the delivery and come inside with me?" he asked.

She stepped back and tossed a black rectangular object at the guy's chest. Was that his wallet? Hermes chuckled. It sure was.

The guy caught it, a baffled expression contorting his features as the woman dangled his watch in front of his face.

"How about you learn to treat women with respect?" She dropped the watch into his hand, turned on her heel, and marched toward the gods' house. Pausing at the foot of the porch steps, she took a deep breath and blew it out hard, shaking her head as if to chase away thoughts of the confrontation.

Hermes rose to his feet, unable to fight his smile. She was a courier and a thief. *Be still my heart.*

"Great form," he said as she climbed the steps and stopped in front of him. "The wrist flick when you snagged his wallet was a nice touch. Very professional."

She opened her mouth like she wanted to say something and then cut her gaze to where the college boys stood moments ago. The sidewalk lay empty, the boys having retreated inside to lick their wounds after being outwitted by a woman.

"Why did you give it back to him?" he asked.

"I didn't need it." She tugged her phone from her

pocket again and swiped the screen. "Are you Cole Black?"

Cole was Hades' alias among the mortals. Z didn't want them to use their real names—anonymity was supposedly best—but Hermes couldn't bring himself to go by any name other than his own. What was the point?

"I'm with NOGS," she continued, pronouncing it like a word rather than letters, "here to pick up a delivery."

He laughed. "Surely your employer doesn't allow you to call your company NOGS. No respectable courier service would go by such a name." N-O-G-S would be the correct pronunciation. It had to be.

She pointed at the letters on her shirt. "NOGS."

He pursed his lips, wanting ever so badly to press the issue—NOGS was the most ridiculous name he could imagine—but she seemed agitated, almost as if the mere presence of a god didn't faze her. *Intriguing.* He stepped toward her. "Who taught you to pickpocket?"

She cocked her head, giving him a curious look. "No one."

"Your skill level speaks otherwise."

Her brow arched. "Is Mr. Black inside?" She held his gaze, moving closer and placing her hand on his shoulder…the distraction. Her other hand reached behind him as she brushed past, and, had he been mortal, he might have missed the faint sensation of his wallet lifting from his pocket.

But Hermes wasn't mortal—nowhere close—and he did, in fact, sense her trick. Before her lithe fingers could claim their prize, he spun, clutching her by the wrist with one hand, while simultaneously whisking her necklace free and clutching it in his fist. "Nice try, dearest, but no one steals from the god of thieves."

"Oh, you're a god, are you?"

"In every sense of the word." He held up her necklace, and her eyes widened briefly before she scowled.

"Give that back." She reached for it, but he jerked his hand away.

"Tell me who taught you to pickpocket."

"None of your business. Hand it over."

Hermes grinned. Would she speak to him this way if she knew who he really was? Gods, he hoped so. The woman was fierce. She reached for the necklace again, and he shook his head. "Tit for tat," he teased.

Was that a growl emanating from her throat? Aphrodite have mercy, where had this woman been all his life? "My father, okay? Now give it back."

He gazed at the pendant lying in his palm. A locket. What secrets had she concealed inside? "What's your name?"

"Kathryn."

"Well, Kathryn of N-O-G-S, your father taught you well."

"I'm so glad you approve of my upbringing." Her voice dripped with sarcasm. "May I have my necklace back now?"

He tossed it to her, but his infatuation with the intriguing Kathryn caused him to miss his mark. The necklace sailed above her head. She jumped to catch it, but as she landed, her ankle twisted; her butt hit the railing, and she tumbled backward off the porch. *Whoops.*

"Kathryn!" He rushed toward her, leaning over the rail in time to see her land on her feet as gracefully as a feline. "Are you okay?"

"I'm fine." She clasped the locket around her neck, dropping the pendant down the front of her shirt as she returned up the steps. "Are you Cole Black or not? I've got a job to do."

"Indeed you do. Cole is inside."

"Thank you." She rang the bell, and Hermes returned to his seat in the wicker chair, staring out across the road, while watching the alluring Kathryn from the corner of his eye.

Hermes—and all the gods—had been attracted to plenty of mortals over the eons. He'd always had a soft spot for travelers, traders, couriers, and thieves… but something about Kathryn appealed to him on a deeper level. It almost felt as if a thread of his fate had been woven into hers and only now that he'd met her had it been pulled taut.

Crazy, he knew. As if the Fates would send him a soulmate after all these millennia. No, this was a case of a man being attracted to a beautiful woman. Nothing more.

Hades answered the door, and Kathryn's gaze swept over his tattooed arms before meeting his eyes. He was brooding, as usual, but she wasn't fazed by him either… which made her all the more attractive in Hermes' eyes. She didn't cower in the face of raw power, which meant she must be powerful herself. A witch, perhaps?

"I'm Kathryn from *NOGS*." She glanced at Hermes, a playful smile tugging on her lips as if she said it as a word just to irritate him.

Oh, game on, my little herald.

She glanced at her phone again. "I'm looking for a Mr. Cole Black."

"That's me. Here's the package." Hades handed her the same envelope he'd tried to shove off on Hermes earlier. "And here are the instructions. Do exactly as it says here, and do not, under any circumstances, attempt to follow the receiver inside."

Kathryn took the paper and scanned the instructions. "Your secret knock is 'Shave and a Haircut'? Seriously?"

Hades tapped the rhythm on the doorjamb. "If you expect her to answer, yes."

"Wait." She shook her head, staring at the page. "I've heard of this place. It's deep in the swamp, past the bokor's cottage. Someone actually lives there?"

Hades' nostrils flared. He wasn't used to mortals questioning him. "There will be a boat beneath the tallest cypress tree. Take it to the cabin, knock, and wait for her to answer."

"The deadline is in half an hour. I can't—"

"It's more important than you can imagine. Get the package there on time, return with a signature confirmation, and I will double your fee…in cash."

Kathryn's eyebrows rose. "You got it."

Hades closed the door, and Kathryn turned toward the steps, chewing her bottom lip as she stared at the envelope. "Shit. Hermes himself couldn't deliver this package on time."

That sounded like a challenge. He rose to his feet. "Want to bet?"

She shook her head. "Excuse me?"

"Hermes, herald of the gods, protector of travelers, and god of speed, at your service." He bowed.

She scoffed and descended the steps. "Right. If you're Hermes, then I'm Pandora."

"You've already got boldness and cunning. Let me give you hope." He followed her down the stairs and stopped in the driveway, gesturing to his Ducati. "I've also got the fastest motorcycle ever created. I can get you there on time."

She narrowed her eyes at Hermes and then cut her gaze toward his bike. "All right. But if you try anything funny, I won't hesitate to claw your eyes out."

Hermes laughed. He would love to see her try. Seriously, that would be hot. "You have my word. No funny business."

Not yet anyway.

CHAPTER TWO

Kathryn Gataki, a calico cat shifter who unironically went by Kat, wasn't known for making good decisions. Hopping on the back of a bike with a delusional man who thought he was a god would have come as no surprise to anyone who knew her.

She did think twice about doing it, and that had to count for something. But with an extra hundred dollars on the line—money that would pay her bills —she threw caution to the wind and accepted the helmet "Hermes" offered her.

"Will you at least tell me your real name?" She slipped it on her head and swung her leg across the seat, settling behind him.

"I told you, it's Hermes." He winked over his shoulder.

Well, she supposed it was possible the name was genuine. She did go to school with an Athena growing up, so why not? "Do you have a last name?"

"Swift, but I only use it when necessary. Most of the time, Hermes is enough."

"I bet." She gripped the sides of his shirt, hesitating to get any closer. He was tall and lean, with a swimmer's build and tailored clothes that fit him like he was born in them. He had clean-cut, dark brown hair, a short, neatly trimmed beard, and hazel eyes that made her feel like he was looking into her soul every time he caught her gaze.

He was too hot for his own good…or…for her own good, it seemed. He was either batshit crazy and really thought he was a god, or he was just having fun. If it were the former, she'd be kicking herself for being attracted to yet *another* weirdo. If it were the latter, it wouldn't hurt to see how far he'd take the game.

Hermes started the engine and revved it, the deep melodious rumble drowning out the sounds of revelry from the French Quarter a block away. "You need to hold on tighter than that, dearest. This thing packs a punch."

Kat slid her arms around his waist, pressing her front into his back. He was solid and warm, and he smelled like he'd just stepped out of the shower and dressed in freshly washed clothes straight from the dryer. It was a good thing she had a helmet on. Otherwise, she'd have been tempted to press her nose into his shoulder and breathe in his fresh, clean scent. *Please don't be a weirdo.*

"Here we go." He pulled out onto the street and practically flew toward the highway. Seriously, if the bike had wings, they'd have been airborne.

Wind whipped against her bare arms as she tightened her grip on his body. A chuckle vibrated from his back, and she could imagine the same flirtatious smile he'd greeted her with on the front porch. Her pulse sprinted, her own lips tugging into a smile as he poured on the speed. *What a rush.*

The scenery blurred around them, and he wove in and out of traffic like the other cars weren't even on the road. She should have been afraid. They had to be traveling at least one hundred miles per hour, but the exhilaration of their pace overshadowed any other rational emotion she might have felt.

Maybe this guy really was the god of speed. If so, what was he doing in New Orleans?

When the call came in to make the last-minute delivery, her boss came straight to her. She overheard him tell Mr. Black that he'd send his fastest courier, but what he really meant was he'd send the one most used to shady dealings: Kat.

NOGS was a courier service for the supernatural, and much like humans, more than a few paranormal bad seeds had planted themselves in The Big Easy. Most of her coworkers were in their teens or early twenties, using the job to pay for college or magic school. They hoped to be done with NOGS as soon as possible, so taking on dangerous clients wasn't high on their to-do lists.

This job came with hazard pay—all the shady dealings did—so Kat jumped at the chance to make some extra cash. Rent was due, and she was still paying off her sister's medical bills.

At the thought of her sister, her mind tried to sink into the dark place, but she bit her lip and yanked it back to the present. She had a scrumptious man, possibly a god—wouldn't that be something?—between her legs. Better to focus on that and save the wallowing in guilt for tonight.

This particular delivery had sketchy written all over it. Her boss gave her the address of the pickup, and that was it. No delivery location. No timeframe. Just the name Cole Black and an address. If she'd known she'd be taking his package deep into the swamp, into an area even the Voodoo Mambo refused to go, she'd have thought twice about accepting the job.

Of course, that was probably the precise reason her boss neglected to give her the information. Kat was tough. She knew how to fight, and she almost always landed on her feet, thanks to her feline side. But nothing could protect a cat shifter from the black magic surrounding her destination.

Well, nothing but a god…

Hermes slowed his bike to a normal speed as he exited the highway and turned down the narrow dirt road. Kat started to ease her grip, but he was still going at least sixty, and the bumps and dips on the uneven path jostled her bones, making her bite her tongue. "Ow!"

The bike skidded to a stop, and he took off his helmet, the wings fluttering as he set it on the seat in front of him. "Are you okay?" Concern etched lines into his forehead before a mischievous grin lifted one side of his mouth. "Did I go too fast for you?"

Kat took off her helmet and shook out her hair, trying to ignore the way his playful smile made her stomach flutter. What had she gotten herself into? "The speed was exhilarating. I bit my tongue when you hit a bump."

"Will you survive?"

She laughed. "I think I will."

"Good. We'll have to walk from here anyway. The path is getting too narrow." He slid off the bike and offered his hand.

She took it, not because she needed his help, but because she already missed the feel of his sculpted muscles pressed against her. She hadn't allowed herself an ounce of pleasure since her sister died, but she'd be one foolish feline to deny the way her body responded to being near him…especially her below-the-waist area. *Down, kitty. You don't know anything about this guy.* Though, she wouldn't mind starting with what was underneath those perfectly tailored clothes. *Purrr…*

Hermes cocked his head. "Are you sure you're okay?"

"Yeah. Why?" She tucked her hair behind her ear.

"You were making a weird sound. Were you vibrating?"

Oh, crap. Way to let the cat out of the bag. "No, I was not. I just had a…tickle in my throat I was trying to clear."

She let out a nervous laugh and took off down the path. Her dad was an honest-to-gods cat burglar. He shifted into feline form to sneak into homes and hotels to steal. Not the best role model for an adolescent, but Kat was fifteen when her human mother passed away from the same cancer that took her sister last year. She was lucky her estranged father took her and Camilla in at all. Cami was only five at the time, and she wasn't even his daughter.

He was good to them, though, and he taught them plenty of street smarts. And Rule Number One was *never reveal your magic.* You'd be surprised the information a cat could glean when no one knew she was a shifter. She'd have to be more careful around Hermes. Something about him brought out her animal side.

Her chest started to rumble again, but she shut it off and continued her trek down the dirt trail into the swap.

"What kind of supe are you?" Hermes jogged to catch up.

"Who says I'm a supe?" She cut her gaze toward him but kept walking.

"You work for a supernatural courier service. A human wouldn't have the balls to make the kinds of deliveries you do."

She stopped in her tracks and turned to face him, fisting her hands on her hips. "The balls? Are you insinuating that men are braver than women because a couple of peanuts in a flesh sack dangle between their legs?"

He laughed, and a single dimple formed on his left cheek, right above his beard. "Not at all. Forgive my crude analogy; hanging around a bunch of bikers is starting to rub off on me."

I could rub you off. I bet I could make you scream my name too. Gah! What was it with this guy? Her hormones hadn't worked this hard since…well, she couldn't remember that far back.

A cold shower was in order as soon as she got home… After a round with Big Joe, her trusty vibrator. She made a mental note to pick up batteries on her way to the apartment.

Hermes fought his grin, but mirth danced in his hazel eyes. He tilted his head, giving her a quizzical look, and her stomach dropped down to her toes.

Holy catnip. She didn't say any of that out loud, did she? Surely she didn't tell this gorgeous specimen of a man, whom she'd just met, that she would jerk him off. Yes, his smile—and everything about him— was disarming, but Kat had an arsenal of experience.

When he didn't say anything, she cleared her

throat and replied, "You're forgiven. Don't let it happen again," and she continued down the path.

"You're really not going to tell me what kind of supe you are? I told you I'm a god."

God of lust, maybe. "Perhaps I'm human."

"I doubt they'd send a human to make a delivery for a god."

Twigs crunched beneath her shoes, and a crow cawed from somewhere in the trees. "Cole Black is a god now too? He doesn't look like a deity. What's his dominion? Tattoo parlors?"

He chuckled. "With that kind of sass, you must be a witch."

"Sure, let's go with that."

The ground softened the deeper into the woods they trekked, the solid earth turning to mush, as if they were walking on a sponge. When they neared the bokor's cottage, the hairs on the back of her neck stood on end. Luckily, the hair on her head didn't react the same way. If she were in cat form, she'd have been a fluffball.

"Who lives there?" Hermes asked, and she realized she'd stopped to stare at the dilapidated shack. Peeling white paint had turned green with age, and the front porch sloped downward as if the ground were trying to swallow the place and take the resident to hell where he belonged.

"A bokor. He's a Voodoo practitioner who dances with the devil. Black magic, murder, mayhem. We should keep moving." Kat shivered as she picked up her pace. *Hansel and Gretel* may have been a German fairytale, but the bokor here was keeping the story alive. Only, his adventures didn't involve children and ovens. He'd take anyone at any age, and he preferred bonfires. *This* was why she was getting hazard pay to deliver a damn envelope.

"Maybe we should say hello and leave an offering as we pass? It's nice to see a religion where people still worship their deities." Hermes started toward the cottage, but Kat grabbed his arm and dragged him away.

"This isn't ancient Greece. Trust me, you do not want to say hello to a Voodoo man who practices the dark arts."

"Another time then." He flashed that killer smile and followed her toward the small boat docked at the edge of the swamp.

Towering cypress trees created a canopy over the rickety pier, their branches dappling the sunlight that reached through to the soft ground, and the scents of mud and decaying foliage drifted on the air.

She put one foot on the pier, testing it with her weight. It gave slightly, but it felt sturdy enough to hold her, so she padded across it. Hermes stood on the bank as she stepped into the wooden boat.

"You're coming with me, right?" she asked.

"Do you want me to?" Something about the way he said it made it sound like he was asking about more than the boat ride. How could a man be so intense and yet so casual at the same time? He wasn't a big guy, but he exuded strength and power. He was quick with a smile, yet he held an underlying serious-ness, like an old soul.

Hermes was an enigma, but she refused to get sucked in by his mysterious charm. Well, she refused to let him know he was pulling her in, anyway. "You're my ride home, so yeah." She gestured to a seat in the boat as if she were impatient. She wasn't. His superbike had gotten them to the swamp with plenty of time to spare, but she couldn't let her interest in him show.

Her father's Rule Number Two: *Don't trust anyone.* People—even gods—always had an angle. She highly doubted he was helping her out of the kind-ness of his heart.

"You are an intriguing woman, Kathryn of N-O-

G-S." He dusted off the seat in front of her and sat down.

"It really is pronounced NOGS…and Kathryn is fine." She yanked the cord on the outboard motor to start it and then steered them out into the swamp. "Is this boat always unlocked? It would be easy to steal."

Hermes gave her an appreciative nod. "I like the way you think, *Kathryn*." The emphasis he put on her name made her shiver. He said it like the word belonged to him. "This boat is cloaked in magic. Only those Hades wants to see it will ever know it's there."

She blinked. "Hades? God of the underworld, Hades?"

"Oops." Hermes shrugged. "I should have said Cole, shouldn't I? We started this motorcycle club more than a year ago, and I still have trouble keeping up with everyone's pseudonyms."

She chewed her bottom lip, narrowing her eyes and studying him. Could he be serious about this god business? It would explain how fast he got them here and why he wasn't the slightest bit scared at the mention of a bokor. It would also explain why her feline was trying to convince her she was in heat. *Down, girl. I mean it.*

"I counted twelve motorcycles in the driveway at your house," she said.

Hermes nodded. "One for each Olympian."

"For each… You're saying Zeus, Ares, Aphrodite…all the gods are staying in that house with you?"

"Z, Warrick, and Addie. Yes, they're all there."

"And Cole Black is Hades? I'm making a delivery for the god of the dead, and the god of thieves is helping me?"

"I'm also the god of language, travel, and speed, among other things. Nothing so important as the sun or moon, but…" He clenched his jaw like the thought bothered him. "Yes, that is exactly what's happening." He pointed to a dock in the shade of a willow tree. "There's our destination."

She navigated toward the pier. "Wait. Aren't you the messenger god too? If what you're saying is true, why didn't you deliver this package?"

He tossed a loop of rope around a cleat, securing the boat to the pier. "I'm on vacation. We all are."

"Then why are you helping me?"

"It's my nature to help people." He paused, cocking his head as he studied her. "And you fascinate me."

She sat in the boat as he climbed onto the dock.

There was no way this guy could be telling the truth. He wasn't Hermes. His real name was probably Herman or Herbert or something, and he called himself Hermes to be cool. This was insane.

Or was it?

Dad's Rule Number Three: *Trust your instincts.* She had no idea why, but her gut told her he was telling the truth. "The Olympians came to Mardi Gras for vacation?"

"Indeed, we did." He offered his hand, and she accepted, allowing him to steady her as she stepped out of the boat.

As they made their way to the bank, he gestured to a shack in the trees. The tiny building was made of unpainted wood, and it had a splintered front door. Seriously, this thing was no bigger than an outhouse. It could have held two people standing, one sitting. Surely she wasn't delivering a package to someone on the john.

"Please tell me this isn't a magical roll of toilet paper." She pressed the envelope to her chest, feeling it as if it would suddenly be squishy like Charmin.

Hermes just laughed, so she strode to the door and did the secret knock. Would Hades really be so careless as to use the most common rhythm, though?

That would be the first thing people tried if they knew they needed a special knock.

She stepped back, but no one answered the door. "What is this place, anyway? I don't think they're home."

"Try the knock again. Maybe she didn't hear you."

"You're kidding, right? The building can't be more than ten square feet. How could she not hear me?" She tapped out the rhythm to humor him, but again, no one answered. "So much for meeting my deadline. I've got five minutes to deliver this to a person who isn't even home." She reached for the doorknob.

"I believe your instructions said not to go inside under any circumstances."

Kat hesitated, but she turned the knob anyway. What could she say? She didn't like being told what not to do. "It's locked."

Hermes stepped toward her, pursing his lips as if he wasn't sure of his next move. He narrowed his eyes, looking thoughtful for a moment before he spoke, "I have a key." He unhooked his bracelet, and it magically morphed into a golden staff complete with wings and two snakes spiraling up the stick.

A caduceus. *Hermes'* caduceus. *Holy hairballs.*

"What is this place?" Her voice came out as a whisper.

"Give me the package. I'll take it inside and get the signature you need." He took the envelope from her trembling hand. "You seem like a woman who can keep a secret."

She swallowed hard and nodded.

Hermes pressed his lips into a thin line. His gaze was intense, but he finally nodded in resolve. "If Medusa had answered the door, she may have invited you in. She adores the flesh. That's why your instructions said not to go inside."

"Medusa? I don't understand."

"Wait here." Hermes tapped his staff against the door, and it swung open. "This is an entrance to the underworld. Don't make me regret telling you." He stepped through the door, and it slammed shut behind him.

Kat's mouth hung open as she stared at the closed door. An entrance to the underworld? Right outside New Orleans? *No fucking way.*

Pressure built in the back of her eyes, and she clutched her locket—her *sister's* locket—in her sweaty hand. There had been an entrance to the underworld right under her nose all this time!

She gripped the knob and slammed her shoulder against the splintering door, but the damn thing was as solid as steel. "Come on. Open up." She jiggled the latch, ramming her other shoulder into the door with all the force she could muster. It still didn't budge.

Dropping to her knees, she examined the metal handle, looking for a lock to pick, but it was smooth. There was no sign of any locking mechanism, which would have made total sense if she'd paused to think about it. It was a door to the fucking underworld. It was locked with magic, obviously.

And Hermes' staff was the key.

Her mind spun, the plan hatching inside her brain without her even consciously thinking about it. If she could get that key, she could get inside. If she could get inside, she could find her sister in Elysium and rid herself of the guilt she'd been carrying around her neck like a lead collar for the past year.

She could take her the locket and finally apologize for ignoring her pleas. All Cami had wanted was her damn necklace. It held a picture of Kat on one side, their mom on the other. If Cami had been wearing it when she died, she'd have it with her in her spirit form in the underworld. But Kat had been too selfish to go out in the rain and get it from the car, where she'd left it after her last doctor appointment.

Cami had been sick for a year, and Kat had spent every waking moment taking care of her, trying to nurse her back to health. She'd driven her to doctor appointments, brought in Reiki healers, and seen specialist after specialist, racking up a massive amount of medical bills. She had all but given up her own life for her sister, and in one act of selfish rage, she'd undone all the love she'd given Cami during her illness.

Her last conversation with her sister rolled through her mind as she sank onto a fallen tree trunk. She'd been tired after working all day, taking Cami to the doctor on her lunch break, only to return to work right after. Rent was due, and she didn't have enough money to pay it and the electricity. Her boss had yelled at her for being late on a delivery; her nerves were shot, and she wanted nothing more than to take a hot bath and go to bed. As Kat had tucked her sister into bed, Cami had grasped her neck, her frail fingers shaking as she slid her hand down to her chest.

"I left my locket in the car," she'd said. "Will you get it for me?"

"It's raining," Kat had replied. "I'll get it in the morning."

"Please? I like to keep you and Mom close while I sleep."

The fatigue and stress had gotten the better of Kat, and she'd snapped, saying words she could never take back. "You've got me close to you every fucking day. My entire life revolves around you. I'm working this crap job that doesn't pay shit because you don't want me to steal, and I'll be stuck paying your medical bills long after you're gone. I think you can manage one night without your precious locket. Give me a fucking break!"

She remembered it like it was yesterday, the awful words forever burned into her mind. She'd ignored her sister's dying wish and had been a complete and utter bitch. The fact she didn't know Cami would die that night didn't matter. Hell, maybe her tantrum was what killed her.

Kat had tried everything she could think of to apologize. She'd hired more than a few psychics to summon Cami's ghost, but her sister had already moved on. After the seventh one couldn't contact her, Kat had given up that route and looked into hiring a necromancer to bring her back.

She'd have to pay an arm, a leg, and her left boob to acquire their services, though, and she was doing good to make ends meet. Not to mention—as her roommate convinced her—dragging Cami back from Elysium so she could apologize would be selfish. Who knew what a spirit would go through making the transition back to this realm against their will?

Kat would have to go to Elysium herself to make amends.

The question was…how would she get the staff? It was unlikely a god would let a mortal borrow a magical artifact, but it wouldn't hurt to ask. Of course, her father would tell her just to take it, but she'd made a promise to Camilla. Kat swore she'd get her life straight and never steal again. She couldn't break one dying wish to fulfill another.

But she had to do something…

CHAPTER THREE

"It's about time you came out of the pit, Medusa. I was beginning to think you didn't want to get paid." Hermes handed the gorgon the envelope, and she snatched it out of his hands.

"*I* was beginning to think I *wouldn't* get paid. It wouldn't be the first time a god betrayed me." She signed the receipt and shoved it back toward him while the snakes on her head hissed up a storm.

Hermes took the paper, and Agnes and Vern hissed in return. Medusa's snakes never did get along with his, but who could blame them? They fed off her bitter, angry energy since they were attached to her scalp and all.

"The world is safe for another month?" He winked, which earned him an irritated glare.

"As long as I keep getting paid. Now, get out. I've got a tortured soul to punish."

He took his time on the return trip to Earth, mulling over Kathryn of NOGS and the strange emotions stirring in his soul. He had enjoyed the way her soft curves felt pressed against his back on the drive over way more than he should have. It had been a while since he'd indulged in the pleasures of the flesh. Perhaps he should give in to the temptation and seduce her.

He paused on the bank of the River Styx and kicked a stone into the obsidian water. The moment the rock pierced the surface, the water sizzled, steam rising in a column as it disintegrated the stone.

"What'sss wrong?" Vern slithered in a circle around the staff. "Medusa get under your ssskin?"

"Nah, she's all bark and no bite."

"Until she turnsss you to ssstone."

He booped Vern on the head with his index finger. "Which is why I don't look her in the eyes, my friend."

"Don't be ssstupid, Avernusss," Agnes said. "He's brooding over the woman."

"Brooding?" Vern whipped his head toward Hermes. "Why brood? Just turn on your godly charm and ssseduce her."

Agnes scoffed. "Typical male responssse. His trouser snake already standsss at attention around the woman. He doesn't need any help from you."

Hermes shook his head. "No worries, Agnes. Seduction isn't the way to go with Kathryn." Sure, he wanted his fingertips to memorize every dip and curve of her voluptuous body, but he wanted to start by learning her mind. Getting to know her soul.

She was cautious, not fawning over him the way most women did, and he liked that about her. Being in the presence of a deity didn't intimidate her or make her go wild with desire.

He'd told her too much, shown her more than he should, but he couldn't help himself. For the first time in his existence, he strangely felt the need to prove himself to a mortal. To...dare he say it? To impress her. *Zeus almighty, what in Hades' realm is wrong with me?* He'd spent enough of his life trying to prove his worth to the Olympians...and to himself. *Get caught stealing in your first act as a god, and you never live it down.* Now he found himself with the insatiable need for Kathryn's approval too.

After making his way to the exit, he ran his hand through his hair and held his caduceus up so the snakes could see him. "How do I look?"

"Like a cougar ready to pounccceee," Vern said.

Agnes shook her head. "Like a Greek god."

"Good." He tapped the staff against the exit door and stepped into the Louisiana swamp. Agnes and Vern returned to their positions and stilled, appearing to be made of solid gold like the rest of the caduceus. They only ever spoke to him.

Kathryn sat on the trunk of a fallen tree, and she shot to her feet when his gaze met hers. As she smiled, his heart slammed once against his chest before melting into putty. *Good gods.* He was in trouble.

"Delivered and signed, right on time." He offered her the receipt. "Here's your signature confirmation for Hades…I mean…Cole."

"Thank you." She took the paper, but her gaze locked on his caduceus. "Is that really the key to the underworld?"

He straightened his spine. "Indeed, it is. In addition to my many other duties, I'm also a psychopomp. I can deliver souls to their final destinations."

"Wow." She moved toward him, but the look of awe in her eyes wasn't for Hermes; it was for his staff. No, not the one in his pants, unfortunately. "Are there others?" she asked.

"Sure. All the reapers have keys, but none are like this." What would it take for her to look at *him* that way? Why did he need her to?

"Can I touch it?" She caught her bottom lip between her teeth.

Now his trouser snake really was standing at attention. This woman was magnificent. He hesitated. *Of course*, he hesitated because no mortal had ever touched his staff. Well, not the one in his hand. He really needed to drag his mind out of the gutter.

Z would blow his top if he found out about this, but Hermes couldn't help it. He wanted, no, *needed* to please Kathryn. He held the caduceus toward her, and she ran her fingers across the golden wings. The moment she touched it, her arm hairs stood on end, her body reacting to the magic.

Oh no. The magic. Her hand grazed the ball on top of the caduceus, and her lids fluttered before slamming shut. He'd forgotten to warn her about the *other* magic his staff possessed. The sphere put people to sleep when they touched it. *Whoops.*

He caught her around the waist before she could eat dirt and tapped the staff against her arm, instantly waking her.

"Whoa." She blinked, resting a hand on his chest

and gazing into his eyes for a moment. Then she sucked in a sharp breath as if she'd just realized his arms were wrapped around her, and she stepped away, looking at him accusingly. "What did you do to me?"

"I didn't do anything. It was—"

"Cut the crap, god-man." She crossed her arms. "One minute I was looking at your caduceus, and the next I was in your arms. Is that why you volunteered to bring me out here? Because you thought you could get into my pants?"

Her words stung, but he kept his expression neutral. "You have my word I was not trying to seduce you."

"No? What happened, then?"

"You touched my ball."

She scoffed. "I did no such thing. How dare you insinuate I would go anywhere near—"

"This ball, dearest." He pointed to his staff. "It puts people to sleep on contact."

"Oh." She pursed her lips, cutting her gaze between the caduceus and him.

Agnes and Vern would never let him hear the end of this. It was probably taking all their strength not to break character and laugh at him. He transformed the staff into a bracelet and hooked it around his wrist.

"We'd better get you back to Cole so you can get your bonus."

They walked side by side up the trail toward his bike, Kathryn brooding and Hermes fighting his smile. She had spirit. Any other woman would have swooned to find herself in the arms of a god, but not Kathryn.

"I'm sorry for accusing you," she said as they approached his Ducati. "The stories I've heard about the gods suggest you're all horny as rabbits, so I assumed…"

"Who's to say we're not?" He stopped and faced her. "I would never disrespect you in such a way, Kathryn. I merely caught you before you fell."

A tiny smile curved her mulberry lips. "Thank you, and you can call me Kat. That's what my friends call me."

"Are we friends now?"

"I'd like to be."

"As would I." He turned and continued down the trail. Friends was a good start. An appropriate place to begin with someone this captivating. He could control his "horny rabbit" urges until she was ready for them.

"Do you ever take living mortals into the underworld?" she asked.

"Why on earth would a mortal want to visit Hades' realm? They'll get plenty of the place once they die."

She shrugged. "A field trip, maybe?"

He laughed. "Absolutely not…unless it's been ordered by Zeus, Hades, or Poseidon. What those three say, goes. Otherwise, the living stay in their own realm. It's one rule that can't be broken."

"What if a mortal took your caduceus? Could they use it to get in and out?" She was full of questions, wasn't she? Hermes could appreciate her inquisitive nature.

"They could get in, sure. Getting out might be an issue. The underworld is like a labyrinth with dead ends and plenty of pitfalls that could trap someone there for eternity. I wouldn't advise trying it, not that anyone could take it from me. No one—"

"Steals from the god of thieves?"

"Precisely."

"What if someone did, though? What would the punishment be for stealing from the god of thieves?"

"Good question. I suppose, if a mortal actually pulled it off, congratulations would be in order. How could I be angry with someone who bested me at my own game?"

He slowed as they reached the so-called bokor's

cottage, and an elderly man with leathery skin and bloodshot eyes stepped onto the slanted porch. He had a scruffy gray beard and hunched posture, reminding Hermes of the troll in the *Three Billy Goats Gruff* story.

Kat stiffened, sidling next to him and clutching his arm. Whether it was because she wanted his protection or she was trying to hurry him along, he couldn't tell.

"Who dares trespass on my land?" The bokor's voice was gravelly, which was also very troll-like.

"He certainly fits the classic fairytale villain image to a T, doesn't he?" Hermes whispered in Kat's ear before addressing the man, "It is I, Hermes, god of travelers. What offering have you for me, old man?" Hey, if the bokor wanted to be stereotypical, so could he.

"Hermes, don't." Kat tugged on his arm as the man held up his hands and whispered something under his breath. "He's about to curse us."

"I'm a god. He can't curse me."

"Well, I'm not." She widened her eyes and tugged him harder.

"Good point."

A ball of energy formed in the bokor's extended hands, and just as he threw it at them, Kat screamed.

Hermes grabbed her around the waist once more and whisked her away in the blink of an eye—he was the god of speed, after all—setting her down in front of his Ducati.

"How did you…?" She closed her eyes, inhaling deeply as she shook her head. "You're a god. Never mind."

"My apologies for provoking him. I didn't mean to scare you." He took her helmet from the enchanted side pannier and handed it to her.

"I wasn't scared." She pulled it onto her head, buckling it under her chin. "Not much anyway."

"Ready to go?" He put on his helmet and swung his leg over his bike, settling in the seat.

"Can I drive?"

He laughed. "You want to make it back alive, don't you?"

"I suppose." She climbed on behind him.

"No one has ever dared drive my bike, not even the other gods. It's simply too fast."

"Can't blame a girl for trying. Thanks for bringing me out here."

"My pleasure." He had enjoyed her company more than he thought imaginable. So much so that he'd been careless. "Do me a favor, dearest, and don't let the other Olympians know I allowed you to touch my staff. It's forbidden."

She wrapped her arms around his waist. "But I'm allowed to touch you?"

"Only with my permission, which you have, dear Kat. Anytime you want." He started the motor and sped back to his house.

CHAPTER FOUR

Kat couldn't fight her smile as she climbed the stairs to her shared apartment. Cole…er… Hades had made good on his promise to double her delivery fee in cash, and she was able to pay her share of the rent plus have a little extra to splurge. On the way home, she bought a bottle of red wine for herself and a liter of O-negative for her roomie, Deirdre.

The sun had just set, so she let the door swing wide open since she didn't have to worry about frying her vampire friend. Deirdre lounged on the couch with two satyrs playing video games—her boyfriend Nick and an older, gruffer-looking guy Kat had never seen. The distinct scents of body odor and barn animals reached her nostrils, and she cringed. *Please don't let this be another setup.* Cats and goats were not a good match. She'd told Deirdre this several times, but the vampire refused to accept it.

"Hey, Kat." Deirdre rose to her feet and rested a hand on her hip. She wore a pink catsuit with knee-high patent leather boots, and her blonde hair hung in ringlets down to her shoulders. Her blue eyes sparkled with her smile, and she had the kind of cheerful personality that could make even the gloomiest ghost happy. Who knew the undead could have so much life?

Her gaze locked on the bottle of blood in Kat's hand, and she strode toward her. "What are we celebrating? Did you get a promotion? A new job? Wait…did you get laid?"

Kat laughed and closed the door. "I paid the rent."

Deirdre pouted her lower lip and followed her into the kitchen. "That's not fun. Important, I guess, but not fun."

"And I suppose the smelly satyr on the couch with Nick is your answer to my no fun problem?"

"Peter?" Deirdre curled her lip. "C'mon. Even I know better than to try and set you up with Big Billy Goat Gruff. He's way too old. Have a little faith in me."

Kat took two wine glasses and filled them with

their respective drinks. "Good. Because I met someone…"

"Ooh! Someone you're interested in? That's new." She sipped the blood and closed her eyes. "Mmm… Thanks for this."

"You're welcome."

"So, what's he like?" She motioned with her head toward the dining table and settled into a chair. Nick and Peter kept their gazes glued to the television, their thumbs furiously jabbing the controllers as they murdered CGI zombies on screen.

"He's a god." Kat sank into the seat next to her friend.

"Uh-oh." Deirdre winked. "Already joined him in the sack?"

She took a drink of her wine, reveling in the way it warmed her throat on the way down. "No, I did not sleep with him. I met an actual god. Hermes."

Deirdre's brow furrowed. "You mean the man who's dressing as him in the parade? I thought the Krewe of Hermes didn't roll for a few more days."

"It doesn't, but I'm not talking about him. I met the real deal. The god from Olympus himself. He helped me deliver a package to the underworld."

Deirdre laughed, but when Kat arched a brow, she said, "Wait…you're serious?"

"I am."

Peter's spine straightened, his head cocking as if he were eavesdropping. Maybe eavesdropping wasn't the best word. Their entire living and dining area consisted of one open room, so it wasn't like he was listening with his ear pressed to the door, but still.

Kat bit her lip. Maybe she shouldn't have said that in front of the guys. Then again, they were satyrs. If any species of supe was familiar with—and believed in—the gods, it would be satyrs.

"You seriously went to the underworld?" Deirdre gasped. "I hope they paid you extra for a trip like that."

"I got hazard pay, and Hades gave me a big fat tip, which I used to pay the rent and buy our celebratory drinks."

The vampire's mouth fell open. "You met Hades too?"

"I did."

"Are you sure you're not yanking my chain? I mean, the gods aren't really real, are they? They're just legend."

"Hermes did things only a god could do." She leaned forward and lowered her voice. "He let me touch his staff, and I could feel the magic in it."

Deirdre arched a brow. "I bet you could."

Kat laughed. "I'm talking about his caduceus."

"Uh-huh. Sure." She winked. "What's Hades like? Is he hot? I bet he's smokin'."

Nick cleared his throat and paused the game.

Kat shrugged. "If you're into brooding alphas with lots of tattoos, sure."

"Who isn't? That's exactly my type. Just look at Nick." She blew a kiss to her boyfriend.

Kat wasn't. She didn't have a type, but if she did, Hades most definitely wasn't it. Honestly, she hadn't been attracted to anyone in more than a year…until today. Hermes was confident…borderline cocky… but he lacked the macho alpha male crap that always turned her off. He seemed genuine, jovial even. And the way he looked at her made her feel *seen*.

But he had something she needed. She'd have to lay her romantic interest in him aside if she wanted to complete her mission. "I need some advice."

"Don't play hard to get. If you want him, go after him. Supes like you don't live forever, and you're getting awfully close to forty. No offense, hun, but you don't have time to waste."

Kat closed her eyes for a long blink. "That's not what I meant, Dee. I need to figure out how to steal his caduceus."

Deirdre blinked. "Come again? You're going to steal…from a god?"

"Hear me out." Kat lifted her hands in defense. "Hermes is a psychopomp, and his staff is a key to the underworld. If I can get my paws on it, I can get into Elysium, find Camilla, and apologize. I can give her the locket so she'll be at peace."

Deirdre sipped her blood, watching Kat over the rim of the glass. "I'm sure she's at peace without it."

"So *I* can be at peace too."

Her roomie let out a low whistle. "You've been hitting the catnip a little too hard, hun. I know you've supposedly got nine lives and all, but…stealing from a *god?* Are you insane?"

"This guilt has been driving me crazy for a year. You talked me out of hiring a necromancer, but I'll be the one crossing into another realm this time. I have to do this."

"Why don't you just ask him to take you? I'm sure if you batted your lashes and turned on your feminine wiles, he'd say yes."

"He said he can only take a living mortal to the underworld if Zeus, Hades, or Poseidon order it, and there's no way in all of Olympus I could convince one of them. I have to take it from Hermes."

Deirdre tapped a finger against her hot pink lips.

"He's a god, right? What if you gave him an offering in exchange for his services?" She wiggled her brows. "There's one thing you can offer him that'll be fun for you too."

Kat rolled her eyes. "I'm sure he can get any woman he wants with a snap of his fingers. Sex with me won't be enough to convince him."

"It wouldn't hurt to try…"

"Kat's right. She has to take it." Peter stood, and his hooves clomped on the hardwood as he walked to the table. Unfortunately, his unpleasant aroma intensified with his approach.

Kat tried not to inhale too deeply as she shot Deirdre a pointed look. "See? But I need a plan. No one has ever successfully stolen from Hermes."

"He told you that himself, didn't he?" Peter scratched his rump before sinking into a chair. *Gross.* "Old Hermes has always been full of himself."

"Most gods are." Nick laughed and joined them at the table, dropping into a seat beside Deirdre.

"Y'all know the gods?" Kat asked.

"Hermes and I go way back." Peter's grin revealed yellowing teeth. "You seem smitten with the god of thieves. If he's equally as enamored, I'm sure you'll have no trouble getting his staff."

Kat leaned away from him warily. "Any ideas that don't involve me sleeping with him?"

"I still think you should ask him," Deirdre said.

"He won't do it." Peter shook his head. "Gods never allow mortals to use their instruments."

"Unless they're attached below the belt." Nick snort-laughed.

Kat chewed the inside of her cheek. Maybe her roomie was right. "If I go to the underworld alone, I won't be able to get out. Hermes said it's full of pitfalls and traps."

"Of course he did," Peter said. "He's got a god-sized ego, just like the others, even if he claims he doesn't. He wouldn't want you to know how easy his job is."

She leaned her elbow on the table. That sounded about right. If everything she'd learned about the gods and their perceived self-importance were true, it made sense. Hermes did seem like he was trying to impress her. "But I promised Camilla I'd never steal again."

Peter pursed his lips, looking thoughtful. "It's not stealing if you give it back when you're done. I believe that's called borrowing."

That was true. She could borrow his staff, give the necklace to her sister, and then return it before he realized it was gone. That wouldn't be breaking her promise. But if she got caught…

"I don't want to anger a god. What would he do to me if he found out?"

The old satyr waved his hand dismissively. "Hermes never gets angry. If anything, he'd be impressed."

Hermes had told her that himself this afternoon, hadn't he? That he'd congratulate the mortal who could best him at his own game. Her knee bounced beneath the table as the gears turned in her mind. She could do this. It would be like one last hoorah before she hung up her sticky paws for good.

She looked at Deirdre, adrenaline coursing through her veins at the idea. "I'm going to steal Hermes' caduceus."

Deirdre shrugged. "Okay. What's your plan? Sneak in when no one is home and grab it?"

"He keeps it with him everywhere he goes. Most of the time, he wears it as a bracelet. It only turns into a staff when he takes it off."

"That should be easy enough to lift. I've seen you take plenty of jewelry off people without them knowing. It's such a fun party trick."

"That won't work. I tried to lift his wallet, and he caught me."

"But you're such a good thief. No one ever catches you on that one."

"He's the *god* of thieves. I'll have to go under-cover. I'll shift to cat form and prowl the premises. With any luck, his bedroom window will have a ledge, and I can watch him. He must take the damn thing off to shower at least."

"So you *are* going to sneak in and take it?"

"Cat burglar style." She could do this. Of course she could; it was in her blood. Why had she ever doubted herself?

Peter smiled and crossed his arms, leaning back in the chair. "May I offer a bit of advice?"

"I'll take all the help I can get."

"If touched, the sphere on the top of his staff will put a person to sleep instantly."

"I know. I accidentally touched it this afternoon."

Peter arched a brow. "If he catches you in the act, it works on gods as well."

"Hot damn." Her plan was ready. She lifted her glass in a toast. "Reconnaissance this evening, and tomorrow night, I'm 'borrowing' Hermes' staff."

"Can I come with you?" Deirdre asked. "I've never tasted ichor, but I hear it's divine."

Kat laughed. "Seriously? You call me crazy for

wanting to steal from a god, but you think it's okay to try and *drink* from one?"

"A girl can dream."

⁂

Hermes had made it back to the rental house with Kat just as the gods were leaving for the first event on Athena's itinerary: a parade. Kathryn had received her bonus and went on her way as if the delivery she'd made was par for the course and not an errand for the gods.

He'd almost asked if he could see her again, but for the first time in his existence, he feared rejection. Sure, other gods had been rejected over the millennia, but not Hermes. He didn't want to end up like Apollo, relentlessly chasing after a nymph for eons, so he simply waved goodbye as she walked away. He'd find her again, and then the games would begin.

Truth be told, his fear was unfounded. With his good looks and jovial personality, everyone liked him. Of course, the Olympians treated him like he was their little brother rather than an equal, and it worked for him on Olympus. Not here, though. He was attempting to set up boundaries on Earth, and he'd started when he refused to deliver Medusa's paycheck to the underworld.

He paused and scrunched his brow. He had refused, but then he'd done Hades' bidding anyway, hadn't he? *Gods dammit.* Well, it was a start.

He pushed the thoughts aside as the Olympians gathered with the mortals on St. Charles Avenue to watch the festivities. The looks on the other gods' faces made Hermes smile. Every one of them appeared happy, even if they were trying not to show it.

Well, every one of them except Hades. He was still grumbling about Hermes entering the under-world in a mortal's presence.

"You seriously whipped out your staff and used it right in front of her?" Hades' voice boomed above the noise of the crowd, and his glowering gaze could have turned a mortal to stone. Not literally. Only Medusa had that power, but Hades was scary enough when he wasn't mad. Right now, he looked terrifying.

A drunk woman giggled as she approached Hermes. She reached a hand toward him like she wanted to pet him, but when he cocked his head, she put her hands on her hips instead. "I'd like to see you whip out your staff." She licked her lips as her gaze dropped to his pants.

"Perhaps another time, love." Hermes winked, and she shivered…a typical reaction for any mortal woman.

Well, any woman except Kat.

"I told you Medusa wasn't answering the door," Hermes said as the woman walked away. "You said yourself she'd quit and allow the damned souls to escape if she didn't get paid. What was I supposed to do?"

Hades clenched his teeth. "Tell the courier to keep knocking. Medusa would have answered eventually."

"Then the delivery would have been late, and Kat wouldn't have earned her bonus."

He crossed his arms, flexing his biceps. "So? Why do you care?"

Hermes shook his head. He couldn't explain why. He didn't know the answer himself. "She's trustworthy. No need to worry."

"She better be. You're lucky I haven't told Z about this."

"You can tell him." Hermes shrugged. Z might scold him like a naughty child, but that would be the extent of his wrath.

"Tell me what?" Zeus moved toward them and crossed his arms, matching his brother's posture.

Hades puffed out his chest and flexed even harder. "Hermes has a hard-on for the delivery girl, and he whipped out his staff right in front of her."

Zeus laughed. "She was impressed, I hope?"

Hades grunted. "His caduceus, Z. Get your mind out of the gutter."

"It's not a big deal," Hermes said.

Zeus scowled, the air around him growing electric as his biceps bulged. "This isn't a joke, son. I demand anonymity for a reason. I swear to Gaea, if your mortal causes us any trouble at all, I will not hesitate to strike her down. The last thing we need is word getting out that we actually exist."

Jeez, talk about a look that could turn people to stone. That threat against Kat's life sounded way too real…and it sat heavy in Hermes' chest like a lump of lead. He swallowed hard before composing himself, putting on his happy-go-lucky smile. "Relax, old man. I'm an excellent judge of character, and I can guarantee Kathryn won't cause any trouble."

He clapped Z on the shoulder, giving it a squeeze to reassure him. "I simply helped a messenger with her job. It's what I do."

Zeus's hard glare softened slightly. "I suppose it is. I assume you didn't let her *use* your staff. Not your caduceus, anyway."

"Of course not." She stroked it, but nobody needed to know that little detail.

Hades' face reddened. "She knows where the entrance to my realm is. That's reason enough to strike her down immediately."

Holy hellfire. What had Hermes done? He needed to smooth this over quickly before his infatuation with the alluring Kathryn turned deadly. "Take it easy. You're the one who sent her there in the first place, remember? If anyone should be in trouble for introducing a mortal to the underworld, it's you."

A growl rumbled in Hades' chest. "And whose idea was it to use the courier? If you hadn't put up such a hissy fit about making the delivery, none of this would have happened."

"Nothing did happen. She knows it's the entrance, but the area is guarded by some Voodoo man who strikes fear in the hearts of mortals. You should have seen how she clung to me when we passed his dwelling. She was scared shitless; she won't be returning."

"But—"

"And the door is locked by your own magic. Are you worried a little witch might be able to break in? And what would she do if she did? The underworld has nothing to offer the living."

Zeus rubbed his chin as he watched the exchange. "Hermes has a point. She'd have to wrangle a reaper to get inside, and I can't think of a reason why she would want to in the first place."

Hades' eyes glowed briefly before he regained his composure. "Fine. Have your fun with the mortal but know her life is on the line. If anything goes wrong, I'll take her to the tarpits myself, whether Z strikes her down or not. I might even take you to Tartarus along the way."

"Agreed." Zeus nodded. "At the first sign of trouble, the mortal is burnt toast. Do what you will with her, but don't bring her to the house. She might figure out our secret with so many gods in one place."

Whoops. He'd already spilled their secret, but no one needed to know that either. He could trust Kat; he felt it in his soul.

Hades huffed through his nose and walked away, and Z made his way to a hotdog vendor.

"Hermes, this was the best idea you've ever had." Dionysus slung his arm around Hermes' shoulders. His breath smelled of red wine, and the glassy look in his eyes said he'd hit the bottle long before they claimed their spot on the parade route.

"Enjoy yourself, my friend. The mortals still love the god of wine here."

Hermes pushed his conversation with Z and Hades out of his mind and turned his attention to the parade, marveling at the mortals' ingenuity. Massive floats, at least forty feet long, rolled down the center of the street. Many were adorned with glittering papier-mâché flowers and animatronic animals, but the one that lit up Dion's eyes was covered in grapevines. Plump purple fruits the size of beach balls flowed over the sides of the trailer, and a twelve-foot-tall bottle of wine served as the centerpiece.

"This is fabulous." Dion took a swig from his can. "If mortals took the time to worship us like this year-round, we might still be on Mount Olympus."

A marching band followed the wine bottle float, and Hermes joined Dion in a dance as the mortals blasted a jazzy tune. Then, the next float arrived…

"Hold up." Dionysus froze. "Is *that* what they think I look like? I swear to Zeus, I'll smite them all. Watch me turn their wine into toilet water. We'll see how they like that!" He started to climb the fence separating the parade from the spectators, but Hermes pulled him down.

"C'mon, man. It's not *that* bad." He held in his laugh. It *was* that bad. It really was.

In reality, Dion had a full head of thick, dark brown hair and a well-toned, muscular physique. He was a handsome man, like all the Olympians, but the massive sculpture the mortals had created to depict the god of chaos was anything but. He was nearly as wide as he was tall, and the double—no, triple—chin reached all the way to his chest. His toga barely covered his round belly, and his laurels rested atop a hairless head.

"How can you say it's not that bad? I bet your parade won't feature you as a fat, bald man."

Probably not. Even after all these millennia, the mortals' view of Hermes hadn't changed much. They still liked to render him with winged sandals, which he never wore anymore, but he was otherwise shown as a lithe, agile athlete.

"Check out your facial expression, though. Look how happy they made you. And those nymphs dancing around your feet up there seem just as entranced with you as they are in real life."

"Yeah. I guess that's true," Dion grumbled.

"We haven't shown ourselves to the mortals in eons. It's natural for them to get a few things wrong about us." But thank goodness there wasn't a parade for Zeus. Hermes could only imagine how the big guy would react if they got his image as wrong as they got Dion's. He'd probably strike it with lightning and set the whole procession ablaze.

"You're right." Dionysus nodded. "At least they tried. I'm going for another drink. You want one?"

"Nah. I'm good." His mind was too preoccupied with thoughts of Kat, and he didn't want to dull the experience with wine.

In addition to being a yes man—which he was trying to change—Hermes had always been a now man, living in the moment, not concerning himself with what the future may hold. But he couldn't shake the feeling that something else was at play here, and he found himself imagining a future with the alluring Kathryn of NOGS.

He shook his head. He hardly knew the woman. And yet...

A visit to the Fates was in order. He had to know if his destiny was tied to hers, or if he just needed to get laid and get over himself. As luck would have it— and Hermes was the god of luck, so it was always on his side—the Fates had set up shop in the French Quarter when Zeus ordered the closing of Mount Olympus.

Why wouldn't they? The old hags fit right in with all the witchcraft, Voodoo, and magic in this city.

He slipped away from the crowd... Well, it was impossible to get away from the crowds during Mardi Gras, but they did thin out the deeper he got into the

Quarter. He steered clear of Bourbon Street, choosing instead to walk down Royal at a mortal's pace. Quaint two- and three-story buildings painted blue, yellow, or brown lined the street, and eclectic shops and art galleries occupied the first floors. Cheerful wreaths and masks in purple, green, and gold—the colors of Mardi Gras—adorned the windows, giving the area a festive feel.

Most of the stores he passed were closed for the evening, but A Twist of Fate was always open. The Fates never slept. How could they? They wove the fabric of the universe. Without them, the world would fall apart.

He paused outside the wooden front door to read the sign. "A Twist of Fate. Potions, lotions, and the world's most accurate tarot readings." Hermes laughed. Mortals definitely got their money's worth when they had readings here.

A bell chimed as he stepped into the shop, and the scents of patchouli and sage greeted his senses. Clotho sat behind the counter, but she didn't look at him when he walked in. She didn't need to; this Fate was blind, but she *saw* everything. She wore a frumpy black dress with a strand of glass beads around her neck, and her thinning hair was combed over like a middle-aged mortal with self-esteem issues.

"Hermes of Olympus." Her voice sounded scratchy and deep, like an old witch's. "To what do we owe the pleasure?"

"Greetings, Clotho. Are your sisters here? I need some information."

"Yes, yes. We're always together." She rose from her seat and motioned for him to follow her into the back of the store. "You caught us on a slow night. The tourists would rather spend their money on booze than a glimpse into their futures this time of year."

"I bet."

Clotho drew aside a beaded curtain and gestured for Hermes to enter the next room. Inside, he found Lachesis and Atropos sitting at a wooden table. Lachesis shuffled a deck of tarot cards, and her sister flashed him a gnarly smile.

"Greetings, god of thieves. We've been expecting you." She waved a hand at a chair, and it slid out from beneath the table. "Sit, sit."

Hermes accepted the seat, and Clotho joined them. "What can you tell me about Kathryn of NOGS?" he asked.

Lachesis laid out a spread of cards, nodding as she examined them. "Your heart has opened," she said.

"Strange emotions are stirring…" Atropos added.

"In your soul," Clotho finished the sentence. The

Fates were sisters, but not in the traditional sense. They almost seemed to share a psyche, always knowing what the others were thinking and talking in creepy rounds like this. It must have been quite a show for the mortals to watch them work.

"I know what's happening in me. I need to know about her. Is she my destiny?"

Lachesis turned over a few more cards and licked her cracked lips. "The thread was spun many moons ago…"

Clotho tapped a card. "Before she was born…"

"It's up to you to weave it into place."

"I knew it!" Hermes' heart swelled with joy. He'd watched thousands of mortals find their soulmates over the millennia, and now it was his turn to experience such bliss. "Why did it take so long?"

Clotho arched a brow over her milky eyes. "Do you dare…"

"Question the Fates?" Atropos lifted her magical scissors—the ones she used to cut a thread, thus ending a mortal's life on Earth.

Hermes' throat thickened at the warning. He couldn't live with himself if he was the reason Kat's life was cut short. Hades and Zeus had already threatened him. He didn't need to add a third peril into the mix. "Of course not, ladies." He turned on the charm. "I would never question your process. Please, forgive my insolence."

Atropos put her scissors away. "Go now."

"The thread is in place…" Lachesis said.

"But it is not without knots."

Hermes rose to his feet and bowed. "Nothing worthwhile is ever easy to obtain. Life would be dull otherwise."

Clotho's wrinkled hand clutched his. "She will take more than you are prepared for."

"I'll give her anything she wants."

CHAPTER FIVE

Kat parked her Vespa two blocks away from Hermes' rental house and ducked into an alley before shifting into her feline form. As her paws hit the pavement, her fur stood on end, and she flicked her tail, waiting for the godsawful skin-crawling sensation to dissipate.

She loved her calico, with her orange and brown spots dotting her pristine white fur, but every time she shifted from one form to the other, it felt like she needed to jump out of her hide. Goosebumps covered her from head to toe, and her muscles contracted beneath her skin, freezing her for a moment or two before she regained full control of her body.

It sucked big smelly hairballs, but there was nothing she could do about it. She was half-human, so she had to deal with a few hiccups in her magic. It was nothing she couldn't handle. Luckily, every time she shifted, her clothes and whatever was in her pockets were absorbed by the magic. When she returned to human form, everything would be in its place, so that was cool.

She slunk up the sidewalk toward the house and slipped through the wrought-iron fence into the back yard. Though calling it a yard was an understatement. A fountain bubbled in the center of the grassy plaza, and stone benches and sculptures sat beneath the massive magnolia trees that provided shade in the sultry summers.

She jumped onto the ledge of a first-floor window and peered inside at the modern kitchen. Did gods even eat? Of course they did. She'd read about the grand feasts they had on Olympus, so they had to at least eat ambrosia and magical grapes.

The big question was, did they poop? Or were their bodies one hundred percent efficient, and they had no need to? Surely, since they were gods, they could enjoy the pleasures of food and drink without the annoying trips to the bathroom that went with it, right?

She'd always imagined the Olympians as celestial beings made of light or energy or air...not really physical. But Hermes had felt solid and warm pressed against her on the bike, like a living, breathing man.

Now is not the time to contemplate the man's existence. She leaped to the ground and hopped onto the next ledge. This one was a bedroom, but the lights were out, so she couldn't see much. Most likely, it was the master, and that probably belonged to Zeus.

She scoped out all the downstairs windows but saw no sign of Hermes. Aside from the single light burning in an upstairs bedroom, the place seemed deserted. Thunder clapped, and she mewled as she gazed at the darkening sky. Static in the air made her fur fluff, which meant the bottom could drop out any minute. She'd better get a move on.

Up to the balcony I go. A lattice of vines climbed the wall near her destination, so she flexed her claws and began her silent ascent. She reached the balcony and balanced on the railing, creeping closer to get a better view. A pair of French doors stood closed, but their glass panes allowed her to see most of the room inside.

A queen-sized bed draped in a dark blue duvet stood against one wall, and a wooden dresser with a giant mirror sat adjacent to it. On top of the dresser… Was that a winged helmet? It sure was. *Hot damn.* This was Kat's lucky day. It was a good thing too, because none of the other second-floor windows had ledges. If this wasn't Hermes' room, she'd have been shit outta luck.

On the far wall, a door stood closed, and as it swung open, steam wafted out. Hermes appeared, wearing nothing but a fluffy white towel around his waist, and Kat nearly fell over backward at the sight of him. "Sculpted like a Greek god" was a saying for a reason. *Damn…*

She shouldn't have stayed there gawking at him. If their roles were reversed, she'd have called him a creeper, but she couldn't tear her gaze away from all that perfection. He was lean like a long-distance runner, which would have made sense if she'd stopped to think about it. He was the messenger god, duh. He had broad shoulders and a well-defined chest that tapered into a narrow waist.

And those abs. *Yum.* His towel was slung low on his hips, giving her a view of that scrumptious V that pointed to his sweet spot. Wait… Why was she here again? Oh, right. She needed to steal from the god of thieves.

He turned toward the dresser, which put his back to her, and tossed the towel onto a chair. *Oh, my.* His backside was a sight to see, but the mirror… It showed her *all* of his front. *Holy Hades.* Those ancient Greek sculptors did not do him justice. *Wowzers.*

A mewling sound emanated from her throat as he bent over to tug a set of blue flannel pajama pants from a drawer. As he put them on, she drifted forward, her feline insisting on a closer look. But she lost her balance and screeched as she tumbled head over tail off the railing and onto the balcony floor. Contrary to popular belief, cats did *not* always land on their feet. At least, this time she didn't.

She hit the wood with a *thud*, smacking her side and sending sharp pain ricocheting through her entire body. Growling, she righted herself as the French doors swung open and Hermes appeared on the balcony.

"Hello there, beautiful. Fancy meeting you here."

Kat hissed, arching her back and scooting backward until her butt met the railing. He'd spoken to her like he thought she'd understand. *Holy crap.* Did he know who she was? No, he couldn't possibly. She never told him she was a shifter; he thought she was a witch.

Calm down, Kat. You've got this under control. Breathe…

He squatted in front of her and held out his

hand. "I'm not going to hurt you. Come here. It's okay."

She relaxed her stance, letting him approach. She could play the role of a house cat if it would get her inside and near the caduceus. His hand brushed the side of her cheek before he ran it down the length of her back, and damn it if she didn't enjoy that a little too much.

A drop of rain splashed on Hermes' bare wrist as he scratched under her chin. No bracelet. His caduceus had to be in his room somewhere. He gazed up at the sky as fat droplets plopped down on them, soaking into Kat's fur. She shook and meowed. Gods, her calico hated getting wet.

"Let's get you inside before it pours." Hermes scooped her into his arms and carried her in, closing the balcony doors behind him. One of them stuck, and he had to slam it with his shoulder, which made a loud thud as it finally closed.

That could be a problem for her escape plan, but she'd worry about that later. Tonight was simply a reconnaissance mission. She'd find the staff and then figure out what her method of escape would be for the actual theft.

He set her on the bed and sank down next to her,

running his hand down her back. "You know, in some cultures, calicos are said to be harbingers of luck."

She scanned the top of his dresser, searching for the caduceus, but it wasn't there. Maybe he put it inside. If so, she'd have to wait until he slept to do her search. She'd need hands to open drawers.

"I'm the god of luck," he continued, "so it's no surprise I'm receiving a sign of good things to come."

She padded to the head of the bed, and her gaze locked on his nightstand. There it was! The two-foot-long staff lay next to the bedside lamp, the gold softly glowing in the dim light. Yes, indeed, her calico did bring luck, but not for Hermes. She inched closer, fighting the urge to reach out a paw and touch it.

"Careful." He picked her up, cradling her against his bare chest. "They might bite."

Hermes sighed, chewing the inside of his cheek as if contemplating something. Rising to his feet, he stepped toward the door leading to the hallway and closed it, locking her in his bedroom.

Now she'd really have to wait until he slept if she wanted to go home, but that was fine. She could think of worse people to be locked in a room with.

He returned to the bed, sliding his legs under the covers and leaning his back against the headboard. "I can't talk to the gods about this, and Agnes and Vern think I'm crazy." He cut his gaze toward his staff as if he expected it to respond. "Don't you?"

Agnes and Vern? Did he name the snakes on his caduceus? Or maybe it was the wings? How odd.

Meh. So he talked to inanimate objects. He was allowed to have a few quirks, right? She could live with that.

Wait a minute… She didn't need to *live* with anything. It wasn't like they were going to start dating. She'd return his staff when she was done with it, he'd go back to Mount Olympus after Mardi Gras, and she'd never see him again.

Why did the thought make her heart ache?

Hermes cradled her against his chest, petting her and nuzzling his face against her fur. How a person treated animals said a lot about his character, and Hermes had a sensitive side. He was kind and gentle, unlike the men she grew up around. He'd have been her father's gang of thieves' patron god if they'd believed in him. But those men were nothing like Hermes.

"Tell me, Kat." He held her up so he could look into her eyes, and her heart nearly beat out of her chest.

He knew! She was waist-deep in the litter box now. How would she explain her appearance on his balcony? And more importantly, why she stayed in cat form when he brought her inside. Surely he'd realize she was up to no good, and then what?

Hermes cocked his head. "Do you have a name? If you're going to hang around the house, you'll need one."

Thank the heavens! He'd called her cat with a C, not by her name. Though, she might be down to eight lives after that near-panic attack.

He pursed his lips like he was thinking. "I suppose 'Cat' will do. You're a beautiful creature, much like another I know called Kat." He set her in his lap and continued petting her.

Kat eyed the caduceus. This could work. Tomorrow night, she'd return to his balcony. He'd let her in, and she would wait until he fell asleep to steal it. The following morning, she'd head out to the swamp and finally get into the underworld to see her sister.

It was a foolproof plan. Simply thinking about it gave her a spike of adrenaline…maybe too big of a spike. Old Kat always got a high off thievery, but she really had mended her ways. She was simply borrowing this time.

"I saw the Fates today," Hermes said.

Kat snapped her gaze toward him. *The* Fates? As

in the sisters who wove the fabric of the universe? Her eyes must have been wide, because he chuckled as he petted her head.

"Do you believe in love at first sight?" He paused as if waiting for her to answer, so she meowed.

"No, I suppose you don't. Animals are much more practical when it comes to matters of the heart. I didn't believe in it myself—much to Eros's chagrin, by the way—until today."

Today? What on earth was he talking about? She curled into a ball on his lap and gazed up at him. Truth be told, she knew exactly what he was talking about. It was ridiculous to even consider he might mean her, but something deep inside her wriggled with anticipation for him to continue...and, no, it wasn't a hairball. Not this time.

"I suppose it's crazy for me to call it love. I hardly know Kathryn of NOGS, but the thing is...for the first time in my existence, I want to. I want to know everything about her. I can't get her off my mind. Is that weird?"

She stared at him, blinking. *Uh, yeah. You just met me today. I could be a nose-picker for all you know. Or maybe I chew with my mouth open or fart every five minutes.* She didn't do those things...not in front of other people, anyway...but he didn't know that.

Then again, maybe it wasn't so weird. Calling it love? Yeah, that was cray-cray. But, honestly, she wanted to know him too, and she wanted him to know her. *That* was weird.

"Kathryn is beautiful; there's no doubt about that. But there's so much more to it, you know? She's cunning and smart, a thief and a courier. I was so convinced she was made for me, I had to visit the Fates to find out for sure."

Kat swallowed, her mouth going dry at his confession. At least he wasn't solely attracted to her looks. She'd give him points for that.

"They confirmed it. She's meant to be in my life. Now the question is, how do I make her understand?"

Make me understand what? That you think I'm your soulmate? This was too much, too soon. Was she attracted to Hermes? Hell yeah. He was a god. Who wouldn't be? But fate…their destinies being woven together? She was in charge of her own destiny, and some old hags at a spinning wheel had no influence on the choices she made. Kat shot to her paws and jumped from the bed before darting toward the balcony.

"You see?" He followed her to the door. "I'm afraid Kat will have the same reaction if I tell her this." He opened the door wide enough for her to slip through. "I don't want to scare her away."

You just did. And that was a good thing. She needed to tame her hormones and start looking at him as a job. Dad's Rule Number Four: *Never get your emotions involved in a heist.*

"I'll leave it open in case you want to come back. Thank you for listening."

She ran through the door and jumped onto the balcony ledge. Without looking back, she crawled down the lattice and hightailed it away from Hermes and his talk of destiny. If she believed in destiny, she'd have to believe it was Camilla's fate to die before she turned twenty-five—and hers to neglect her sister's dying wish.

Nope. No way. She'd made a bad decision that night, and she was going to make amends...and Hermes was the key to it all.

She paused on the sidewalk and gazed at the house. Destined to be with a god...? Wouldn't that be something? It wasn't like he could take her back to Mount Olympus with him, anyway. She was destined to take his caduceus, maybe, but whatever feelings for the man she had blooming in her heart would die if she didn't water them. And that's exactly what she would do...er...*wouldn't* do.

CHAPTER SIX

Kat's phone chimed with her next delivery assignment, and she swiped open the screen. A red bar sat at the top of the form, which meant the job came with hazard pay. She started to smile about the extra cash, until her gaze landed on the name of the client: Hermes Swift.

Her heart sank. As much as she needed the money, she would have to let someone else take this one. Looking into the eyes of the man she was about to steal from—who apparently thought he was in love with her—wouldn't be a good idea. She had to push her emotions aside if she was going to pull this off.

"Hey, Matt." She knocked on the doorjamb of her werewolf boss's office. "Can you give this one to somebody else? I did a delivery for them yesterday."

"Nope, it's all you." He didn't look up from his computer screen as he typed. "No one else can do it."

"Taylor takes on hazard-pay jobs now. Can I give it to him?"

Matt stopped typing and looked at her. "They asked for you by name. Apparently, they were impressed with your speed."

"C'mon, Matt. I really don't—"

He slammed his laptop shut. "Do you value your job, Kat?"

She fought the urge to hiss at his display of dominance. "Of course."

"NOGS is the only supe-run courier service in New Orleans. Good luck finding a job at a human company with your criminal record. But…if you really don't want to do it, I'll give it to Taylor."

Her nostrils flared as she blew out a breath. "It's fine. I'll do it." She turned on her heel and marched down the hall. Matt was too alpha for his own good. One of these days, she might give in to instinct and show him how sharp her claws could be.

She checked the assignment. Once again, the delivery destination wasn't specified on the form. Who knew where Hermes would be sending her? She steeled herself to face him, climbed on her Vespa, and headed to his house.

He sat on the porch in the same place as yesterday, and he gestured to a chair as she strode up the walk. "Good afternoon, Kat. Have a seat." His smile was warm, and the look in his eyes drew her in, making her stomach flutter. *Not good.*

She straightened her spine. "I'm here to pick up a delivery. I don't really have time to sit."

"What time is your next pickup?"

"Two."

"Well, then, we have a few hours. I'd say that's long enough to sit. Please." He gestured to the chair again, and she eyed the seat.

Maybe she was taking her father's *don't get your emotions involved* advice too seriously. The words Hermes spoke last night weren't meant for her ears. It wasn't fair to judge him for feeling things she wasn't supposed to know he felt. And if she *didn't* know how he felt, she'd have taken no issue with sitting with the man for a bit.

Besides, she fully intended to return his caduceus the moment her trip to the underworld was complete. So, technically, she wasn't planning to steal from him. She would simply borrow it…without his permission, but whatever. The devil was in the details. Perhaps her dad's rules didn't apply in this situation.

As long as Hermes didn't profess his undying love,

they could hang for a few minutes. He was fun to be around…and to look at. Especially naked. She bit her bottom lip. That was a sight she could never unsee, and thank the gods for that. Thank *this* god.

"The messenger deity has hired a messenger." She sank into the chair. "Where are you sending me?"

His smile widened, revealing that adorable dimple and making her fluttering stomach do a backflip. "I was hoping we could go there together."

She arched a brow. "If you're planning to deliver the package yourself, why did you hire me?"

He let out an embarrassed laugh. "I have a confession."

Uh-oh. No more confessions, please. I've heard enough. And damn her heart, but the more she thought about what he'd said, the more she liked what she'd heard…which was utterly ridiculous. She was a thirty-five-year-old calico shifter who could barely pay her rent. Like she would ever fit in with a bunch of immortal gods.

"I don't need you to deliver a package."

"I see." She crossed her arms and leaned back in the chair, eyeing him like she was irritated…which she wasn't. Honestly, just being near the man gave her a sense of contentment she hadn't felt in ages. But he didn't need to know that.

"I neglected to get your phone number yesterday, which made it difficult to ask you on a date. I was hoping you'd have lunch with me." Uncertainty furrowed his brow, as if he was actually worried she might say no. She supposed a god wouldn't be used to rejection.

"Oh, I don't know." Her heart screamed yes, but her mind said absolutely not. Her dad's rules had never steered her wrong, and Hermes was technically her target. She couldn't go on a date with the man and then steal…er…*borrow* from him. *Ugh!* Why was her brain so scrambled? Follow the rules. Don't follow the rules. *Make up your damn mind, you furry feline!*

"You've intrigued me, Kat, and I want to get to know you. I'd like for you to get to know me." He leaned forward, resting his elbows on his knees and clasping his hands. "Gods don't grovel. Please don't make me beg."

The only thing she wanted to make him beg for was *more*. Eros have mercy on her heart.

Her stomach growled, reminding her she'd skipped breakfast this morning. Having lunch with the man wouldn't hurt anything, would it? She could call it another reconnaissance mission. Maybe she could glean some information on the underworld from him. Like how to find Elysium once she got inside. That would be good to know…something she needed to find out before she opened the gates of hell.

"Sure. Why not?"

The man had a smile that could melt the ice off a snowman's ass. "Excellent. Where would you like to go?"

"Definitely not the Quarter; it's way too crowded this time of year. There are some great restaurants on Magazine Street if you don't mind the drive."

"I love driving. Let's go." He stood and offered his hand.

She placed her palm in his and rose to her feet. "Don't you need directions?"

He laughed and shook his head before guiding her down the stairs. Oh, right. He was the god of travel…the one man on Earth who actually *didn't* need to ask for directions.

Hopping on his bike, she wrapped her arms around him and snuggled against his back. His firm muscles felt good beneath her palms, and she fought the urge to slide her hands along the sinew. Yep, rule number four just went out the window. *Crap.*

Hermes wove through traffic like he had the pattern memorized, making the drive to the Garden District way too short. Something about being on the back of a powerful machine, with her arms wrapped around a powerful man, really got her motor humming. It was all she could do to keep from purring.

He parked on the curb at the corner of Magazine and Aline Streets, and Kat led him to her favorite po-boy shop, where they dined on roast beef sandwiches and shared a basket of fries.

"Gods do eat mortal food," she mused as she watched Hermes take a bite of his sandwich.

He looked at her quizzically while he chewed, swallowing before he spoke. "What else would we eat?"

"I don't know." She picked up a fry. "Ambrosia? That's what all the stories say."

His smile faded, and he set his sandwich on his plate. "I haven't had that since the fields were razed."

"Razed?" She took a gulp of sweet tea to wash down her food. "What do you mean?"

He pressed his lips together, cutting his gaze left and right. "I've said too much."

"No, you haven't said enough. Why were the fields razed? Don't you need them? Surely you don't have mortal food imported to Mount Olympus."

"We don't live on Mount Olympus anymore." Sadness softened his eyes. "Zeus shut it all down and moved us to Earth about a year ago. To Seattle, of all places."

"Why?"

He sighed and rested his arm on the table. "No one believes in us anymore."

"I believe in you." She placed her hand on top of his. She shouldn't have. Gods knew she didn't need to get herself involved with him, but she couldn't help herself. He seemed so sad.

He turned his hand over to hold hers. "Let's keep that bit of information between us, yes? Mortals aren't supposed to know." He scoffed. "Not that it matters, when most people believe I'm a myth…but just in case."

"Yeah, of course. You can trust me." She bit her tongue. He most definitely could not trust her. She'd already blabbed about him to her roommate and the satyrs, but she could keep this secret for him.

"I know I can." The look in his eyes said he really believed he could.

A tiny stab of guilt flashed through her chest, but she ignored it. Once she got her hands on his caduceus, she'd be unloading a life's worth of the heavy emotion. She could endure another little pinch.

"Your father taught you to pickpocket. Tell me

about that." He squeezed her hand before releasing it and returning to his sandwich.

"There's not much to tell. My mom had a thing for bad boys, and my dad was no exception. He made a living sneaking into hotel rooms and stealing from tourists. He still does, actually, which is why I haven't spoken to him in five years. A life of crime is not the life for me." Not anymore, anyway.

"If people don't want their things stolen, they should try harder to keep them in their possession."

"That's one way of looking at it." But would he feel the same way tomorrow morning when his caduceus was missing? Doubtful. Once again, the thought of taking the staff sent adrenaline flushing through her system. She couldn't tell if she was excited or nervous…or something else entirely.

"I didn't ask to be the patron god of thieves, you know. The title was bestowed upon me after I stole Apollo's cattle."

She squeezed her eyes shut, giving her head a tiny shake to chase away the excitement. *Chill, woman. You are not going back to your old ways. This is a one-time thing.* "I remember that story. The legend says you were just a baby when you did it."

"I was. It was my first act as a god, and it has followed me ever since." He picked up a fry and dropped it on his plate. "Apollo is god of the sun, Artemis is goddess of the moon. Athena's dominion is war, while Hephaestus is god of fire. And me? I'm the god of thieves, messenger for the important ones."

Wow. This was a side of Hermes she didn't expect to see. "I'm sorry."

"Don't be." His demeanor shifted, instantly switching from troubled to his normal cheerful mood. "I'm happy with my lot in life, and it has only gotten better since…" He flicked his gaze to hers, his eyes tightening as if he almost said something he shouldn't have. "Since we came to New Orleans. But enough about me. Is your mother also in the thieving business?"

"No, she was a waitress. She died of cancer when I was fifteen. My dad stepped up and took me and my sister in. That's when I learned how to steal."

"And your sister? What does she do?"

A familiar ache sat heavy in her chest. "She died of the same cancer that killed my mom. I was…" She inhaled deeply. Why was she telling him all this? Kat rarely spoke of her family to anyone, but something about Hermes made her want to open up and lay it all on him. He seemed like the one person who could handle the weight of her baggage.

"I was taking care of her. She was such a good

person. She wanted to be a nurse." Pressure built in the back of her eyes. It was time to end this conversation before she wound up sobbing on his shoulder. "Anyway, I promised her I'd give up stealing, so I got a job with NOGS. The end."

He wiped the corners of his mouth with his napkin before laying it on the table. "Life has not been gentle with you."

"No kidding."

Hermes rose to his feet and offered his hand. "I saw a bakery three doors down. It's nothing compared to ambrosia, but I hear chocolate can work wonders to soothe the soul. Share a slice of cake with me?"

Well, she'd already shared more about herself than she'd planned to. Splitting a dessert couldn't hurt. "Sure. Why not?"

He didn't drop her hand as they strolled onto the sidewalk, and dammit, she let him hold it. She liked Hermes way more than she cared to admit. Maybe she should try asking him to borrow the caduceus. If he said yes, she could rid herself of the remorse about her sister, *and* she wouldn't be taking on any new guilt. But if he said no, her taking it would be that much worse. Dad's Rule Number Five: *It's better to beg for forgiveness than to ask permission.*

Had she mentioned what a fantastic role model her father was?

Hermes couldn't remember a time when simply holding a woman's hand made him feel this good. Kat had a colorful backstory, her rough life molding her into a captivating character. As they strolled hand in hand down Magazine Street, for possibly the first time in his existence, he wasn't bothered by their mortal's pace. In fact, he enjoyed slowing down with Kat. Perhaps he could even *settle* down.

No, not perhaps. If the Fates deemed it so, it would be…as long as he could get Kathryn on board. Mortals and their pesky free will could be fickle some-times, so he'd have to play his cards right. So far, things were going well.

They stopped in front of Sweet Destiny's bakery, and Hermes gazed at the two-story Victorian painted pristine white with light blue trim. The scents of vanilla and fresh-baked scones drifted on the air.

"Shall we?" He gestured toward the bakery.

Kat glanced at the time on her phone. "You promise you can get me back to my Vespa by one-forty-five? I don't want to be late for my next pick-up."

"The god of speed is never late."

"Well, the courier of NOGS has been before, and then she doesn't get paid."

"Cross my heart, you'll be on time." He drew an x over his chest with his finger.

She looked down at their still-entwined hands and smiled. "Okay then."

Two massive oak trees towered on either side of the front walk, creating a canopy over the yard. As they reached the porch, he held open the door, reluctantly releasing Kat's hand so she could step inside.

A woman with long copper hair and fair skin greeted them. "Hey, y'all. Welcome to Sweet Destiny's. How can I help you?"

Kat bit her bottom lip and swept her gaze over the glass display case. "That devil's food cake looks amazing." Her dark eyes met his, and the thread of destiny in his heart wove a little tighter. "What do you think?"

He would share anything with her. "That sounds perfect. Coffee as well, please," he said to the woman.

They settled at a small table near the window, and Kat leaned her forearms on the surface. "Who takes the souls to the underworld since you're on vacation? I assume people still die when the gods take a break."

"Reapers handle most of the grunt work these days. I'm only called in when a soul is particularly ornery, or it's someone of high importance."

"That's nice that they help you out. It would be overwhelming to be responsible for all the souls by yourself."

Hermes scoffed. "They don't *help* me. I could easily do it all on my own, but I choose to let them reap so they'll feel needed."

She laughed. "Reapers gotta reap."

The woman set a massive slice of cake between them, along with two forks and two mugs of coffee. "Here you go. My name's Destiny. Let me know if you need anything else." She smiled warmly before returning behind the counter, and Hermes glimpsed a single white feather floating to the floor as she strode away. It glittered with magic for a second, and then it disappeared.

"Do the other gods have keys?" Kat asked. "Can they get in as easily as you?"

"Hades does, of course, but I'm the only other one." He sank his fork into the cake and took a bite. The rich, dark chocolate melded perfectly with the creamy, sweet frosting, practically melting on his tongue. "Mmm… This is really good."

Her bottom lip had found its way between her teeth again as she watched him, and something akin to desire sparked in her eyes. At least, he hoped it was desire. There was one way to find out.

He slipped out his tongue to lick a bit of frosting from his lip, and her mouth opened slightly before she closed it and swallowed. Yep, that was yearning in her eyes. *Game on.*

Her brow arched, a mischievous grin lifting one corner of her mouth as she slid her fork into the cake. Her gazed locked with his as she placed a bite in her mouth, her lips closing around the utensil in a way that was obviously meant to make him imagine them closing around something else entirely.

His gaze dropped to the fork as she seductively pulled it out, and she closed her eyes, an *mmm* resonating from her throat as she chewed.

Aphrodite have mercy…

He cleared his throat. "How long have you lived in New Orleans?"

"All my life. What's the underworld like?"

"Depends on which part you mean."

"Elysium."

Ah, of course she wanted to know about Elysium.

Most mortals assumed that was where they'd go when their time on Earth ended. "It's a nice place to spend eternity. The weather is always sunny and warm, and the souls there are happy."

"Where is it?" She took another bite of cake.

"What do you mean?"

"Once you go through the door in the swamp, how do you get there?"

Hermes chuckled. How he enjoyed her inquisitive nature. "Once Charon takes you across the River Styx, you follow the yellow brick road."

Kat crossed her arms, arching a brow. "Seriously?"

He nodded. "It used to look like a grassy path through a forest, but people watch too many horror movies these days, so they're wary of the woods. Nearly everyone is excited to follow the yellow brick road."

"Do people ever get lost on the way?"

He tilted his head. "Why so many questions about the underworld? Are you ill?" If her family members both died of the same cancer, it was possible Kat had it too. A sinking sensation formed in his stomach at the thought.

"No." She shrugged and scraped a bit of frosting off the plate. "Just curious about where my mom and sister are."

The ache in his chest eased. At least he wouldn't lose her to illness. Now he'd have to make sure Zeus and Hades kept their claws off her and he might have a chance at a future with her. "I've not heard of anyone who belonged in Elysium getting lost on their way there. No need to worry."

She licked the frosting from the fork, closing her eyes and inhaling deeply like she was savoring it. "Who knew devil's food cake could be so heavenly?"

Hermes cast his gaze to Destiny, who stood behind the counter, frosting a sugar cookie. "The baker is divine, so it's not surprising."

Kat flinched as if his words had stung, and she straightened her spine. "I guess you're into redheads?" Was that jealousy he detected in her tone? Gods, he hoped so.

He took her hand across the table. "I meant she's an angel, dearest. Her wings are hidden with magic, but I saw a feather fall when she walked away."

"Oh, of course." She lowered her gaze and tried to pull from his grasp, but he laced his fingers through hers before she could.

"I'm into *you*, Kat. I thought I'd made that clear."

She looked at their joined hands before lifting her gaze to his eyes. "You have. With the environment I grew up in, and the men I've dated, you'll have to excuse me. I've been burned too many times."

"I would never hurt you."

She tugged her hand, and this time, he let her go. "That's what they all say."

She lacked trust. He'd have to make a point to prove his fidelity every chance he got.

"We better get back. I've got three more pick-ups today, and I won't be surprised if my boss adds more." She rose to her feet. "Thank you for the cake and coffee, Destiny. It was delicious."

"Anytime," the angel replied. "Be careful out there."

It seemed the place Hermes needed to be careful was in his heart. Kat's mistrust of men must have been the knots in their thread of destiny the Fates mentioned. They also said she'd take more than he was prepared for…

She'd already stolen his heart.

The drive back to his rental house was over far too quickly, and as she slid off the bike, she handed him her helmet and shook out her silky brown hair. "Thank you for lunch."

"Thank you for the company." He put her helmet into the side pannier and set his on the seat.

She stepped toward her Vespa and turned toward

him, tucking her hair behind her ear. While she didn't say anything, she hesitated to leave.

He closed the distance between them. "I'd like to see you again. May I have your number?"

She pursed her lips for a moment before holding out her hand. "Give me your phone."

He placed it in her palm, and she added her name and number to his contacts before handing it back to him.

"I guess I'll see you soon?" she asked.

He leaned toward her, gently brushing his lips to hers. When she didn't pull away or slap him, he went all in, cupping her cheek in his hand and deepening the kiss. She rested a palm on his hip, so he moved closer, sliding an arm around her waist and pulling her body to his.

After a moment or two, she broke the kiss with a quick inhale and stepped out of his embrace. "I'll take that as a yes." Her smile warmed his soul. "I have to go."

"You'll see me very soon. Have a pleasant rest of your day, Kathryn of NOGS."

"You too, Hermes of Olympus."

CHAPTER SEVEN

"I'm more excited about this than I should be." Kat strolled arm in arm with her roomie down Frenchman Street, just outside the Quarter. Street-lights and neon signs in the windows of the clubs illuminated their path, and jazz music drifted on the chilly night air. "Old Kat is rearing her ugly head, so you have to promise to talk me out of it if I *ever* try to pull a stunt like this again."

"Of course," Deirdre replied. "I tried to talk you out of it this time. If things go south, be ready for a great big *I told you so*."

Kat laughed. "I would expect nothing less. Is there anyone you want me to say 'hello' to while I'm in Elysium?"

Deirdre shook her head, and her blonde ponytail

shimmered in the streetlights. "I have a feeling vampires don't make it to that part of the underworld. Our afterlife is right here on Earth."

Brisk February air stung Kat's cheeks, and being close to her cold-as-a-corpse friend didn't help with the lack of heat. But nothing could spoil her mood. Yes, she'd gotten a little closer to Hermes than she'd planned, but that might be a good thing. He was playful, and he loved a challenge…just like her.

He would admire her skill when he found his caduceus missing tomorrow morning. When she returned it, they'd have a good laugh. The god of thieves couldn't hold a grudge against the one person clever enough to steal from him. Kat would get what she wanted, while Hermes didn't have to break any unbreakable rules. It would be a win-win. Tingling adrenaline flushed through her veins again, and she shivered.

Besides, it wasn't like she'd hurt anything by seeing her sister. She'd keep the visit brief, give her the locket and apologize, and then head back to the surface. Then she'd be free to live her life without the guilt. Well, as long as Camilla forgave her. What if she didn't? Hermes might not hold a grudge, but Cami sure as hell could.

A brass band struck up a jazzy rendition of

"When the Saints Go Marching In" on the sidewalk, yanking Kat out of the dark place her mind tried to drag her down to, bringing her back to the present. She was out with her friend to pass the time until she was sure Hermes would be home for the night. *Live in the moment, Kat. Worrying doesn't do a lick of good.*

This part of town, right outside the French Quarter, wasn't nearly as congested as Bourbon Street, but Mardi Gras season always drew a crowd. Hundreds of tourists milled about the area, popping into bars and clubs to get a taste of the local music scene.

"What about someone from when you were human?" Kat asked. "There's got to be *somebody* you'd like to say 'hi' to."

Deirdre tilted her head and paused, thinking. "No, not really."

"Seriously? Not even your parents? No one?"

"They all died so long ago." She rested a hand on Kat's shoulder. "We have to let them go at some point. If you'd lived as long as I have, you'd understand." Her gaze landed on something behind Kat, and her eyes sparkled. "Nick's band is about to go on. Let's grab a seat."

Kat had only seen Deirdre's boyfriend play once. Grunge music wasn't really her thing, and she could only stand hearing "Smells Like Teen Spirit" every so often. But Deirdre had been following the band from gig to gig for the past three weeks, ever since she met her flavor of the month. That left about a week's more time in their relationship, and good riddance when it ended. Kat wouldn't miss Nick's smelly new friend when he was gone…or the scuff marks his hooves left on the living room floor.

She followed her roomie into the bar and ordered a club soda. She'd need to keep her wits about her if she was going to pull off the ultimate theft. It shouldn't have excited her like it did, but she couldn't help slipping back into her old way of thinking some-times. She might as well enjoy the rush, right?

Deirdre slid onto a barstool and spun around to face the band. Her smile was so wide, it showed her fangs, but that didn't matter. Nobody batted an eye at a vampire in New Orleans these days. The city was a hotbed for the undead.

The band started with a Pearl Jam cover, and Kat let her gaze wander over the crowd, taking in the faces and checking out their jewelry and their current states of inebriation. She spotted a man leaning so far forward in his chair his wallet had nearly fallen out of his pocket on its own. His girlfriend had short hair, the clasp to her diamond necklace lying exposed on the back of her neck.

If she were still in the thieving business, they'd be her first targets. She wasn't, though, and while she had no desire to return to a life of crime, she couldn't help scoping out the potential payoffs. Hey, old habits died hard. She was trying her best to be a good girl.

Speaking of payoffs, that group of twelve in the back corner sure had an otherworldly vibe about them. Eight men, four women. Just like the Olympians. A redhead laughed, and as she leaned forward to grab her drink, Kat caught a glimpse of Hermes.

He wore an emerald green sweater, and every strand of his dark brown hair fell perfectly into place. He said something that must have been hilarious, because all eleven of his god-friends busted out in laughter.

Hermes smiled and sipped what looked like whiskey before his gaze flicked toward the bar, landing on Kat. Her breath caught, and her lips curved into a smile of their own volition. She couldn't help it around that man. He made her as giddy as a kitten with a new ball of yarn.

He excused himself from the group and rose to his feet before sauntering toward her with a confident gait. Her pulse sprinted, her inner feline mewling her approval. *Down, kitty. Let him make the first move.*

"Kathryn of NOGS." He leaned an elbow on the bar next to her.

"Hermes of Olympus."

He drifted toward her and whispered in her ear, "It's Seattle now, remember?"

His breath was warm against her skin, making her shiver. "I do, but I thought that was our secret." She gestured to her roomie. "This is my friend Deirdre."

"Nice to meet you." She shook Hermes' hand and gave Kat a curious look.

Kat winked and turned her attention back to the smokin' hot god by her side. "What brings you to Frenchman Street?"

"Aphrod…" He cleared his throat. "Addie wanted to see the headliner here. Apparently, she follows their YouTube channel. What about you?"

"Deirdre is dating the bass player." She gestured to the band on stage.

"Hmm…" Hermes rubbed his chin with his thumb and forefinger. "Then I guess I shouldn't ask if you'd like to take a walk with me."

"You absolutely should ask. I can't stand this music." She glanced at Deirdre, who shook her head and rolled her eyes. "Do you mind?"

"I planned on ditching you as soon as their set

was done, so you might as well." She laughed. "Do your thing, girl."

Hermes held out his hand, and Kat accepted, letting him lead her out of the club and onto the sidewalk.

"It's a nice night," he said as they turned down a side street and ventured away from the crowds.

"A little cold for my liking." Kat scooted closer to him. He was warm, unlike her vampire friend, though finding relief from the chilly wind wasn't the only reason she wanted to be near him.

He wrapped his arm around her shoulders, tugging her against his side. "I forget how the weather affects mortals sometimes. Do you want to go back to the club?"

"No. This is fine. I don't mind it too much." Honestly, she liked being close to him. Being wrapped in the arms of a god beat listening to cover tunes any day.

They walked in silence for a while, and Kat's mind quieted. Being with Hermes, she felt at peace, like she'd finally met a man who understood her on a soul-deep level. He didn't judge her for her past indiscretions and instead accepted her for who she was.

Well…everything he knew about who she was anyway. She'd tell him she was a shifter as soon as she returned his staff. Once this job was done, she'd tell him anything he wanted to know.

He paused on the sidewalk, and Kat blinked, returning to her senses. They stood outside his rental house. All the lights inside were dimmed, and a dozen motorcycles filled the driveway. She hadn't even noticed the direction they were walking.

The wind kicked up, stinging her cheeks, and she shivered, instinctively moving closer to Hermes and resting her hand on his chest. No, it was not a ploy to get him to ask her inside. Cats huddled together to share their warmth in the winter. She couldn't fight her instincts. *Don't judge.*

Hermes wrapped both arms around her and rubbed her back. "Mind the cold too much now?"

"A little bit." Although, standing here face to face with Hermes, his fresh, clean scent filling her senses, the warmth of his body enveloping her, she forgot all about the air temperature.

She tilted her head toward his, and he angled his down toward her, and she couldn't resist. She brushed her lips to his.

He kissed her back, holding her tighter and slipping his tongue into her mouth to tangle with hers. The faint taste of whiskey lingered on his lips, warm and inviting, making her want more.

His beard was soft, and it tickled her cheek as he glided his lips along her jaw before whispering in her ear, "Would you like to come inside?"

She shivered, and it wasn't from the cold. "Won't the other gods be upset if you bring a mortal into their lair?"

He chuckled. "Absolutely. Z will flip his lid…if he finds out." He arched a brow, a playful look dancing in his eyes.

"I don't want to get you in trouble." She cupped his face in her hand, running her thumb across his cheek.

"I live for trouble." He tucked her hair behind her ear. "And the band Addie wants to see doesn't go on until ten. We'll have the place to ourselves for a few hours."

Holy hairballs. A few hours alone with Hermes? She'd have to be one finicky feline to turn down that offer.

Hold up. Think about this. She'd read plenty about mythology. This was what the gods did… they seduced mortals. They fucked like rabbits, and there weren't enough goddesses in all of creation to keep them busy, so they came to Earth to sow their wildly divine oats. There was a strong chance once he had his way with her, he'd be done with her.

Was she up for another *wham, bam, thank you, ma'am?*

She stepped back and swept her gaze down his form. Hell yeah, she was. She'd seen the package, and now she couldn't wait to unwrap it. Of course, he'd probably ruin her for other men. How could sex with a mortal compare to sex with a god? To sex with *Hermes…*

She was about to find out.

"Let's go make some trouble."

His gaze smoldered, and he inhaled deeply, as if just the thought of being with her satisfied him. The man knew how to make a woman feel wanted; she'd give him that.

Taking her hand, he led her up the driveway toward the house. When they stepped inside, she scanned the scene. A sofa and several accent chairs filled most of the living room, and an eighty-inch television was mounted to the wall above the fire-place. Those weren't too hard to unmount, but carrying that sucker down the street without being noticed would be impossible.

A pair of expensive-looking riding gloves sat on the kitchen counter, and… What was she doing? Her plan to borrow Hermes' caduceus was seeping into her mind and triggering her thieving instincts. *Stop it,*

Old Kat. New Kat doesn't do this shit anymore, so you'd best focus on the incredibly sexy god who wants you.

"Not what you expected?" Hermes asked with an amused grin. What was it about his smile that was so…panty-melting?

"Just taking it all in. I've never been in the vacation home of the gods before." Nor had she been this attracted to anyone in her life. Would she find him this appealing if he were mortal? Did it matter?

She slunk toward him, resting her hands on his chest. "I'd like to see more."

He licked his lips. "What would you like to see?"

"Your bedroom for starters. Then we'll see what pops up." She ran her finger down his stomach, stopping just below his navel. Who was seducing whom?

"Right this way." With his hand on the small of Kat's back, Hermes guided her up the stairs. All of the bedroom doors stood closed, and he opened the last one on the right. His room.

She stepped inside, turning in a circle and taking it all in. "Nice. How many bedrooms?"

"Twelve." *Sweet Cerberus,* she was beautiful. She wore a dark red sweater that clung to her curves and skinny jeans that didn't leave much to the imagination when it came to her figure. He hadn't planned on bringing her inside. Hell, he hadn't intended for their walk to lead them to the house at all, but he'd felt pulled here. Like tonight was meant to happen. The knots in their thread of destiny would finally unravel so they could weave a future together.

She ran her fingertips across the dresser. "This place must cost a fortune to rent."

"Gods aren't lacking when it comes to fortunes." He clutched his hands behind his back. *Well, what now, Hermes?* He had her here. She'd made her interest clear, so why was he hesitating?

Because Kat was different. She wasn't some random mortal he'd seduced. She was special, and he wanted to savor her.

"I doubt you lack much at all." She slid her hands behind his neck and kissed him. "But I do hope the god of speed knows how to slow things down in the bedroom."

Oh, she wanted to play, did she? Gods, this woman was irresistible. "Don't worry, dearest. I plan on taking my time with you." He rested his palms on her hips. "In fact, you'll be so thoroughly satisfied when I'm done, you won't remember what century we're in, much less how long you've been here."

She arched a brow. "You're awfully confident in your abilities."

"I'm a god. What can I say?"

"Well, then…" She slid her hands beneath his sweater, and the feel of her warm fingers against his flesh nearly buckled his knees. "I hope you have a special delivery for me, god of heralds."

He chuckled and gripped her ass, pressing his hips into hers. "Unwrap my package and find out."

"With pleasure." Lifting her hands, she tugged his sweater over his head and tossed it aside. Her breath caught at the sight of him—a normal reaction for a mortal woman when she saw a half-naked god—but something in her eyes, something about the way she looked at him, made *him* feel like the one who'd hit the jackpot…and she was fully clothed.

She ran her hands up his stomach, brushing his nipples as she reached his chest, and his core tightened, heat flashing through his entire body and settling in his groin. The simple touch of a woman had never made him feel this way before.

He tugged the hem of her sweater, hesitating long enough for her to change her mind if she wanted to. When she lifted her arms, he slipped the garment off and laid it on the dresser. *Eros, have mercy.* She wore a black satin bra with a tiny golden heart charm between her breasts, and as he traced his fingers along the edge of the fabric, she smiled.

"You're not the only one who needs unwrapping."

"You're so beautiful, Kat." He kissed her, dipping his tongue into her sweet mouth and drinking in her essence. With a flick of his fingers, he unhooked her bra and tossed it onto her discarded sweater, but as he slid his hands around to cup her breasts, his caduceus bracelet brushed her arm.

The *ball* on the caduceus, to be exact.

Kat's lids fluttered, and then she passed out.

"Gods, dammit." He caught her before she could smack her head on the dresser, and he laid her on the bed.

"You guys could have reminded me I had you on, you know," he grumbled as he unhooked the bracelet and returned the caduceus to its staff form.

"And misss the show?" Vern writhed like he was excited. *Fantastic.*

"You ssseemed busssy," Agnes said. "We didn't want to bother you."

Hermes rolled his eyes and touched the tip of the staff to Kat's arm.

Her eyes flew open, and she scowled. "You didn't need to knock me out to get me into bed."

"I'm so sorry. I forgot I was wearing the bracelet,

and the sphere touched you." He held up the staff. "Can you ever forgive me?"

She eyed the caduceus. "Depends on how good you are at making it up to me."

"Challenge accepted. Let me put this somewhere out of the way." The last thing he wanted was an audience while he explored the magnificent creature lying in his bed.

He set the staff on the counter in the bathroom, closing the door before returning to the bedroom. "Where were we?"

Kat smiled seductively. "I think you were about to rock my world."

"Oh, it's on." He kicked off his shoes and took off his pants, standing before her in nothing but his dark gray briefs, his package straining against its wrapping.

She licked her lips as he moved toward her, and when he unbuttoned her jeans, she lifted her hips, allowing him to slide them off her legs. While he was there, he peeled her panties off and stood back to admire her.

"Your beauty rivals that of a goddess."

"That's sweet of you to say." She rose onto her knees and hooked a finger in the waistband of his underwear, tugging him closer.

"It's the truth."

"Mmm…" She palmed his dick, wrapping her fingers around it through the fabric, and he groaned. As her lips explored his stomach, she worked his underwear over his hips and gripped his cock, flesh to flesh.

Holy fuck. As much as he loved her forwardness, if he was going to take his time with her, he'd need to turn this around before her mouth moved any lower. In a flash of godly strength and speed, he pulled from her delicious grasp, whisking her into his arms and laying her on her back in the center of the bed.

She gasped, but then, as he covered her naked body with his, she moaned. It was the most enchanting sound he'd ever heard.

He showered her in kisses, trailing his lips down her neck and across her shoulders, leaving not a single inch of skin uncaressed as he worked his way down her body. Her hands felt like velvet gliding across his back, and when he moved below her navel, she slid her fingers into his hair.

"Hermes?" Her voice was breathless.

"Yes, dearest?" He kissed along her hip bones.

"I know I said I wanted you to take it slow, but if I don't have you inside me soon, I might explode."

He chuckled, blowing a warm breath across her sweet spot and raising goosebumps on her skin.

"Trust me, Kat. You won't regret giving me a little more time."

Flicking out his tongue, he bathed her sensitive nub in wet heat, and she gripped the sheets, twisting them in her hands. When he licked her a second time, her entire body shuddered as a mewling sound emanated from her throat.

"Do you want me to stop?" he asked.

"Oh, gods, no. Keep going."

He returned his attention to her center, slipping a finger inside her and reveling in the erotic noises she made. He could have lain there pleasuring her for hours. The softness of her skin, her sweet scent, her taste… It was almost enough to drive him to madness.

Apparently, she felt the same way. She arched her back, dragging her hands across the sheets and crying out his name as she came. "I need you," she panted. "Hermes, please."

He couldn't hold back any longer. He lay on top of her, filling her with one swift thrust as he slid his arms beneath her and held her tight. With his deep inhale, her intoxicating scent filled his senses, and he lost himself to her.

Moving his hips, he slid in and out, her warm wetness enveloping him like they were made to be together…which they were. She kissed his neck, grazing his shoulder with her teeth before nipping his earlobe and sending warm electricity vibrating through his entire body.

His climax coiled in his core, unleashing at last when she screamed his name once more. As the orgasm subsided, he stilled, wrapping his arms around her tighter and nuzzling into her neck. She held him too, clinging to his shoulders and hooking her legs around his. It seemed neither of them was ready to let go.

Her heart pounded against his chest, beating in time with his own, and as their pulses slowed, he lifted his head. Her smile took his breath away. She may not have been a goddess in the literal sense, but she was the goddess of his heart.

She grazed her fingers across his forehead, brushing a lock of hair aside. "I am *so* glad I ran into you tonight."

He laughed. "You and me both, Kat." He rolled off her, tugging her to his side, and she came to him willingly. A thank you gift was in order for the Fates. They'd done him good this time.

Propping her head on her hand, she traced her fingers down his stomach before running one along his length, making his core tighten with her touch.

"Why did all the ancient Greek sculptors make you so…small?"

"You know how mortals can be. If they sculpted us as endowed as we really are, the men would have been too jealous to worship us."

She nodded thoughtfully. "And the women would have been sorely disappointed with them."

Voices sounded from downstairs before the front door slammed shut, and Hermes sat up quickly. *Damn it to Hades, they're home early.*

"I should go." Kat rose and padded toward her discarded clothes.

"I don't want you to." Hermes followed, taking her hand. "If we stay quiet, they'll never know you're here."

She swept her gaze down his body, lingering on his dick for a moment before she looked into his eyes. "I'm certain I could not stay quiet for long with you." She put on her clothes.

Hermes huffed. He was tempted to say to Hades with it and parade her downstairs, telling the rest of the gods where they could shove it if they had a problem with her. But he had another week and a half to spend in the same house with them, and he didn't want to deal with the drama. Life was getting too good to spoil it.

"Is that a balcony?" She jerked her head toward the door as she put on her shoes. "I can go out that way, and they'll be none the wiser."

"Good idea." He pulled on his pants. "I can get you down safely."

She smirked. "No need. I'm a good climber."

He walked her to the door and dragged it open. It stuck, as old doors tended to do, making a loud scraping sound.

"So much for them not knowing I'm here." She kissed him before stepping onto the patio. "I'll see you real soon."

"Yes, you will."

Kat grabbed on to the lattice running up the side of the house and shimmied down like she'd done it a hundred times. Considering her past occupation, she probably had.

Hermes left the door cracked in case his feline friend decided to return and climbed under the covers. The god of luck just got lucky, and if he played his cards right, she'd be his to keep before this vacation ended.

CHAPTER EIGHT

"You can do this, girl." Kat shook her arms as she paced down the sidewalk toward the secluded alley. The temperature had dropped another ten degrees since her romp in the sack with Hermes, and she shivered as she ducked into the shadows.

Hermes…

She rubbed her arms, smiling at the memory of his hands against her skin. The god of travel knew his way around a woman's body, that was for sure. No roadmap required.

Focus, Kat. Get the caduceus, and you can plan your next vacay in Hermes' bed when you're done.

With a deep inhale, she activated her magic and shifted into feline form. As her paws hit the pavement, the pins and needles skin-crawling sensation paralyzed her and her fur puffed out like a powder puff against the cold.

She stretched, flicking her tail to shake it off, and then padded out of the alley to the gods' home. An upstairs light dimmed, leaving the only illumination inside coming from the television in the living room.

It had been fifteen minutes since she left. That was long enough to not raise suspicion, right? It would have to be. She needed to get in before Hermes fell asleep, and if he was anything like mortal men, he'd be knackered after all the fun they'd had.

Kat scaled the lattice yet again and leaped onto the balcony. She was prepared to scratch at the door to get his attention, but he'd left it open. *How sweet.* There was something special about a man who liked cats, and Hermes was no exception.

As she slunk inside, she found him stretched out on the bed, his arms folded behind his head, and he was wide awake, believe it or not. *Duh, Kat. He's a god. Why would sex wear him out?*

"There you are." He slid out of bed and scooped her into his arms. "I got you a treat. I hope you like cream."

You just gave me some. Her laugh came out as a meow, which made him smile, and that made her stomach flutter. Most men were at their sexiest when they had a brooding, almost grumpy expression, but not Hermes. His smile was what did it for Kat. Well, along with his rockin' bod and exceptional skill in the bedroom, of course. But his smile reached all the way to her soul.

"Don't tell Hera about this. She uses it in her coffee." He set Kat on the dresser and slid a small saucer toward her.

She cringed. He'd watched a few too many *Tom and Jerry* episodes, it seemed. Thanks to cartoons and storybooks, everyone thought feeding a cat cream was a good idea. In reality, most cats were lactose intolerant, including shifters…and especially Kat.

Even in her human form, too much dairy could make her gassier than a hot air balloon, but in her feline form…well, it was best to keep her backside away from open flames.

"Go on. It's okay." Hermes watched her expectantly, and she held in a groan.

While cats and dairy weren't a good combo, the fat and protein in cream made it irresistible to felines. If she didn't drink every damn drop of this, he might suspect she was no ordinary house cat.

Fan-friggin-tastic. She'd have to sleep with the window open tonight, lest she suffocate both her and her roommate with the noxious fumes.

Flicking out her tongue, she lapped up the cream, and her feline savored every drop. When she finished, Hermes picked her up and closed the balcony door. Her stomach bubbled as he returned to the bed, and he set her in his lap, leaning against the headboard and stroking her fur.

Her purring started automatically, and this time, she let it go. She was a cat, for gods' sake. She couldn't help herself. His room was warm, his clean scent intoxicating, and her belly was full. She could enjoy the few minutes left before her intestines began to protest.

And boy, oh boy, were they going to protest.

"I'm in trouble, cat."

Her breath caught for a moment, until she remembered that was what he called her calico.

He scooted further down in the bed and rested a hand on her back. "I'm falling for her, and there's nothing I can do about it. Not that I want to stop myself. I don't. She's an incredible woman."

Her purring intensified. She was falling for him too.

"But I was so caught up in the excitement of finding my destiny, I didn't stop to think about what falling in love with a mortal could mean for someone like me."

She lifted her head and blinked at him, willing him to explain. *Someone like me* could mean anything. Was he a player? Afraid of commitment? Married to a goddess? She tried to remember what she'd learned about the gods in her high school history classes, but she didn't recall Hermes having a wife in the myths. Not that she'd paid all that much attention in school. If she'd known the gods actually existed, maybe she would have.

He sighed, and then, as if he read her mind, he said, "For someone immortal."

Yeah, that could be a problem. He would live forever, and she had less than half a century left on earth. She'd grow old and wrinkly, while he stayed young and smokin' hot. Life was so unfair.

"There might be something I can do." He held her to his chest as he rolled onto his side. "But I'm not sure she'll like my solution."

She curled up next to him, watching his lids drift shut and wanting ever so badly to shake him awake so he'd tell her his solution. The ambrosia fields were razed, so it wasn't like she could drink the nectar of the gods and become immortal along with him. What could his plan possibly be?

Don't concern yourself with details now, Kat. You've got a job to do.

Her stomach bubbled again, the sensation rolling downward toward her backside. *Oh no. Not now.* She tensed, hoping to keep what wanted to come out *in*, but her efforts were to no avail.

She farted.

As if the stench wasn't bad enough, the moment the puff of gas left her behind, her feline instincts made her jump. The movement jostled Hermes, and his eyes opened.

"What spooked you, cat?"

She leaped from the bed and darted beneath it, keeping in character and hoping to Hades the smell wasn't as bad as she thought.

As Hermes sat up, he wrinkled his nose. "I guess the cream didn't agree with you, eh?" He slid out of bed and kneeled on the floor, peering at her beneath the dust ruffle.

She backed up shyly, mortified beyond belief, and Hermes laughed. "It's okay. Now we know. Come on out."

Yeah, right. She just farted in front of the man… no, the god…of her dreams, and he said it was okay? He wouldn't think so if he knew who she really was. Imagine letting one rip while you're snuggled in the sheets with *a god. Jeez Louise.*

But she couldn't hide under his bed forever. She

crept toward him, letting him take her into his arms, and he lay on the mattress again, setting her by his side.

"Hold on." He stood up quickly and paced to the door, opening it just far enough to where it caught on the wood floor.

"I'll leave this cracked for you in case that cream causes more than a little gas." He winked, and her mortification intensified to critical mass. It was a good thing she had fur on her face because she must've been redder than a cayenne pepper.

"Now, even gods have to sleep, so let's get some shuteye, shall we?" He retrieved his staff from the bathroom, setting it on the nightstand before returning to the bed, nestling under the covers and giving Kat's back a stroke.

She lay there staring at him as his lids drifted closed, willing him to fall asleep and trying her damnedest to ignore the fluttering in her stomach. She couldn't tell which sensations were gas and which were her emotions trying to bubble to the surface, but she pushed them aside. There was no backing out now.

The minutes stretched on into what felt like hours. Finally, his lips parted, and he began snoring softly. It was time.

Quietly, gently, she rose to her paws and leaped to the floor. Landing silently—because she was a cat, and she was cool like that—she eyed the caduceus lying on the nightstand. If only her calico had thumbs. Then she could have grabbed the staff and shot out the door without even bothering to open it all the way. Sadly, she was just a normal cat in her feline form, so she had to shift to human to complete her mission.

She called on her magic, and that same tingling, prickling, skin-crawling sensation consumed her as she transformed. On her hands and knees on the floor, she froze, the hairs on the back of her neck standing on end as the awful feeling racked her body.

Thankfully, she didn't groan, and Hermes still lay sound asleep. Rising to her feet, she snatched the caduceus from the nightstand, being extra careful not to touch the ball on top, and tiptoed toward the balcony door.

She tugged on the knob, but the damn thing was more stuck than a peaked-in-high-school jock at a dead-end job. Hermes rolled onto his back, and she froze. His eyes remained closed, though, thankfully, and he smiled softly, probably enjoying his dream.

Kat paused to gaze at his handsome features, but only for a moment. She had to get this caduceus to the gates of the underworld. If she yanked on the door quickly enough, maybe she could get out and down before the sound woke him.

But it wouldn't budge.

She tugged harder, pulling with all her might, and it flew open, scraping against the floor and banging against the wall. Hermes stirred, his eyes blinking as he turned toward her. "Kat? Is that you?" Confusion clouded his features.

Holy hairballs. Oh crap. Crap, crap, crap. This was not good. What was she supposed to do now? She'd been caught stealing from the god of thieves. Hopefully Peter was right about the sleepy ball working on gods, because if it didn't, she'd be screwed six ways to Sunday.

"Sorry." She reached the caduceus toward him, tapping it against his arm.

His lids fluttered. "What?" he muttered, and then he fell asleep.

Man, oh man, she was in trouble now, but there was no turning back. She tucked the caduceus under her arm and shimmied down the lattice.

Who knew how long Hermes would be out? She should have asked him how long the sleep effect lasted when she was quizzing him about the staff. She'd planned to visit her sister in the morning so she didn't have to walk past the bokor's house in the middle of the night, but now she wouldn't have time to wait.

She ducked out of the backyard and strode down the sidewalk at a brisk pace, heading toward her apartment, but she paused before turning the corner. Her stomach bubbled, and a cramping sensation twisted in her gut.

"Oh no." Damn that delicious cream. How could something so decadent fuel her with enough gas to launch her to the moon?

The cramp intensified before cascading downward and releasing like a trumpet playing a long low note. As the blast left her rear end, she thought about Hermes' reaction to her calico when this happened in his room. He was such a sweet, sincere man, and he was kind to animals. He was unlike any man she'd ever known.

She looked at the caduceus. "What the hell am I doing?"

"Ssstinking up the entire neighborhood." One of the snakes on the staff writhed, lifting its head and turning its beady blue eyes toward her. *Sweet serpents!*

"And ssstealing something you shouldn't have taken." The other one's eyes were red.

"You're alive?" She held the staff up toward a

streetlight to get a better view. "Agnes and Vern, right?"

"Hermesss should have been more careful," Blue Eyes said. "It's hisss own fault."

Red Eyes tightened its spiral around the staff and looked at Blue. "How ssso?"

"Don't be ssstupid, Vern." Agnes unwound her top half from the staff, pulling away from Vern. "If he'd kept it in his pantsss, this wouldn't have happened."

Kat's mouth hung open as she cut her gaze between the bantering snakes. "You *are* alive."

Agnes jerked her head toward Kat. "And we've been with Hermes sssince the moment he met you."

"You tricked him," Vern said.

"You knew he wasss falling in love with you, and you used his fragile emotionsss against him." Agnes blew a hard breath through her nostrils.

"I didn't…"

"You seduced him so you could sssteal from him," Vern joined Agnes in glaring daggers at Kat. Hopefully these magical snakes weren't venomous. Their looks were deadly enough.

Kat shook her head, holding the caduceus away from her body just in case. "I didn't sleep with him so I could steal from him."

"The evidence suggests otherwissse." Agnes re-coiled around the staff.

"No, I like him. I mean, yeah, I did trick him, but I slept with him because I'm falling for him too."

"Then why did you sssteal his staff?" Vern returned to his spiraled position.

Kat's shoulders slumped. "I need to take this locket to my sister in the underworld."

"And you didn't ask Hermes to deliver it becaussse…?" Agnes blinked her sapphire eyes.

"Because I…" Why didn't she ask him for help? She'd considered it, but then the idea to take it planted itself in her head, and… "Because I'm selfish."

She'd done it now. Hermes could be *the one*. He said so himself. The Fates said so, and she was taking his most prized possession from him. Sure, he might laugh it off, but that didn't do much for their rela-tionship as a way of building trust, did it?

Way to go, Kat. Living your life just like your old man. She had to give it back. She had to wake him up, tell him what she'd done, and apologize. He'd either help her get to the underworld to see her sister, or he wouldn't, but for once, Deirdre was right. She had to let go of the past and live in the now…and Hermes was her now.

She turned, intent on heading back to the rental house, when a man grabbed her from behind. He yanked the caduceus from her grip, and Kat spun around in time to see Peter, the smelly old satyr, smile.

"Thank you, Kathryn," he said. "Hermes and I have had a long-running feud, and you just helped me get even." He tapped the staff against her head, and everything went black.

CHAPTER NINE

Hermes woke with a start, his lids flying open as he sucked in a sharp breath. Sunlight streamed in through the windows, and as he blinked his vision into focus, gazing at his empty nightstand, a slow smile curved his lips. *Well played, Kathryn of NOGS. Well played.*

He sat up and eyed the empty saucer on the dresser, his smile fading as the reality sank in. Kat was no witch. She was a shifter. A cat shifter. How did he not see the signs? She went by Kat. Her last name was Gataki…which meant "kitten" in Greek…and he could have sworn he'd heard her purring once when they first met.

And that calico… He'd held an affinity for her from the moment he found her on his balcony. Then, he carelessly brought her into his room. Twice. And he confessed his true feelings to her. *Oh, shit.*

That explained why the cat darted out of his room the first time. He mentioned the L-word; it was no wonder she got spooked. It also explained why she so easily scaled the lattice to leave last night. She really had climbed it before.

And she'd come back. Even after his outrageous confession of love—words he'd never have said to her so soon in their relationship, whether the Fates had deemed her his soulmate or not—she had gone on a date with him. Made love to him. Maybe she felt it too. Maybe his confession had rung true, and she knew in her heart they were meant to be, as he did.

Or maybe it was all a ruse.

Swinging his legs over the side of the bed, he ran a hand through his mussed hair. What was she up to? Perhaps she was proving her skill in a playful game. He wouldn't be surprised if she'd taken his *no one steals from the god of thieves* statement as a dare.

And did she ever rise to the challenge. He chuckled. If the balcony door hadn't stuck, she'd have made it without even waking him. Oh, yes. There was no doubt in his mind Kat was his soulmate. How could she not be?

He rose to his feet, picking up his phone and

dialing her number. It rang five times before going to voicemail. "I'm impressed, dearest. You've stolen my staff and my heart. Now, if you'll return the former, the latter is yours to keep. Don't make me chase you." He pressed end and dropped the phone on his dresser.

Actually, he hoped she would make him chase her. Hermes could never resist a good game. Though, he did need to get the caduceus back before Z found out it was missing. He'd rather not anger the god who controlled lightning. Being struck wouldn't kill an immortal, but it sure hurt like hell.

Oh, shit. Both Zeus and Hades had threatened him with Kathryn's life if anything went awry. She had no idea how much danger she was in. How much danger *he'd put her in.* After grabbing his phone from the dresser, he dialed her number again, holding his breath as it rang. He exhaled a curse when it went to voicemail again. He had to find her fast.

He spun on his heel toward the balcony, ready to step out into the morning sun and gather his thoughts, but a piece of paper taped to one of the glass panes stopped him cold. He crept toward the door, his heart sinking into his stomach as the image scrawled on the page came into view.

Panpipes.

"Say it isn't so." He pulled open the door and snatched the paper from the glass. No other writing accompanied the drawing, but words weren't needed. Hermes received the message loud and clear.

Kat was working for Pan, god of the wild.

Walking backward, he plopped onto the bed and stared at the paper in his hands. Centuries ago… millennia, possibly…Hermes had stolen Pan's pipes. It was meant as a joke. Hey, he was the god of thieves; it was what he did, but Pan hadn't found it funny in the slightest.

He'd marched his goat ass up to Olympus—and Pan rarely left the wild, so he must've been pissed—and demanded an audience with Zeus. Old Z didn't take too kindly to demands, but no one had seen Pan in so long, he heard him out. Zeus had scolded Hermes like a naughty child—which, in all honesty, he was, and he wasn't ashamed to admit it. Being naughty was so much fun. Hermes had talked his way out of trouble, returned the pipes, and given a half-hearted apology—the goat god really needed to lighten up—but Pan had sworn revenge.

He'd tried a couple of times, sending whom he thought were skilled thieves to try and steal Hermes' caduceus, but no one stole from the god of thieves. Until now.

Until Kat.

It couldn't be. He refused to believe it. There was no way in Hades' realm a mortal could pull one over on a god like this. Especially not on Hermes. You couldn't trick a trickster.

Yet she had. He crumpled the paper and tossed it on the dresser. He should have seen the signs. She'd been far too intrigued by his staff from the moment he'd shown it to her. She wasn't fazed by being in the presence of a god, didn't tremble at his touch, didn't turn to putty in his hands because she had been planning a heist from the moment they met.

And Hermes had been too blinded by love to recognize the con.

He flopped back onto the mattress and dragged his hands down his face. How could he be so stupid? The Fates hadn't actually said Kat was his soulmate. No, he'd inferred that bit of information because he wanted it to be true. All the sisters had said was that the thread had been spun many moons ago, and it was up to him to weave it into place.

He'd done one hell of a job sewing up his fate, hadn't he? *She'll take more than you're prepared for*, they'd said. She certainly had.

Hermes showered and dressed, but he couldn't bring himself to face the other gods just yet. If they knew he'd been duped—that Pan, of all gods, had used a mortal to trick him—he'd never hear the end of it. He needed to find Pan and get the caduceus back if he wanted to keep his dignity intact, but a strange agony in his chest immobilized him.

Both a burning ache and a sharp stabbing sensation pierced his breast, the pain causing him to curl onto his side in bed. Peculiar emotions swirled inside him, nauseating and dizzy. He'd never experienced such feelings in all of his existence, and his bruised pride wasn't to blame. He loved Kat, and she had betrayed him…fooled him into thinking she might feel the same.

For the first time in his life, Hermes had a broken heart.

A heavy knock sounded on the bedroom door, and he opened his eyes. "What?" he muttered as he rose to a sitting position, planting his feet on the floor.

The door swung open, and Hades stood glowering in the entry. The man was always glowering. "Stop moping like a teenage rock star and get your ass downstairs."

"I'm not moping." He glanced at Hades before casting his gaze to his empty nightstand.

"It's eleven a.m., and you've yet to show your face. What are you doing, then? Jerking off?"

"Shit." Hermes raked a hand through his hair and stood. He had been moping, and it had gone on long enough. If he didn't join the gods in the day's activities, he'd never hear the end of it.

He followed Hades downstairs and found the Olympians around the television. Nodding a hello, he dropped into a chair and rubbed his forehead. What the hell was he supposed to do? He'd been a fool to believe the Fates would send him a soulmate after all these millennia, and now, he'd lost both his staff and his heart.

"It's about time you showed yourself." Z sat in an overstuffed recliner closest to the television.

"Are you okay?" Artemis tilted her head, and her silver hair shimmered as it caught the sunlight filtering through the windows.

"You look like you've been dragged through the pits of Tartarus." Poseidon lounged on the sofa, his brow furrowing as he spoke.

"Or he pulled an all-nighter binge-drinking," Dionysus joked.

"I'm fine." Hermes faked a smile. "What's the battle plan, Athena? Are we heading out?"

"We're skipping the eleven o'clock parade out of

principle," Zeus said. "If all the gods don't get one, a hero certainly shouldn't."

Hermes fought his eyeroll. Yep, there was that ego. There definitely wasn't enough room for it in the streets of New Orleans.

"Look at them all." Zeus nodded toward the television. "Gathering like sheep to worship that idiot."

Hermes opened his mouth, about to explain the parades weren't actually a form of worship, but he thought better of it. He had enough on his plate right now without adding an argument with the gods. He cast his gaze to the screen, where a local news program reported on the festivities.

Crowds in the thousands gathered on the streets, as usual, to watch the massive floats roll through and to catch the beads, doubloons, and other items the krewe members tossed into the horde. The scene cut to a reporter standing on the sidewalk, her dark hair swept back in a twist, concern carving lines into her forehead.

"Nothing like this has ever happened before," she said. "It seems to be some sort of spell affecting people by the masses. Groups of five, ten, twelve people are dropping like flies and falling into a deep, coma-like sleep."

Hermes swallowed hard. This was not good.

The reporter continued, "The source of the magic is still unknown. The first wave of victims began last night, just after midnight. Fifteen people were taken to the hospital after passing out in a bar on Bourbon Street. Doctors were unable to wake them. However, eight hours later, they all woke simultaneously. Tests were run, and no trace of any illness was detected. It has been dubbed The Sleeping Spell, and citizens are urged to stay indoors until authorities can figure out what's happening."

The camera panned across the street to show a group of people lying on the ground with medical professionals tending to them. "Oh no," the reporter cut in. "We're getting reports of another group." The camera panned again to a scene where three others lay unconscious on the sidewalk.

Zeus's nostrils flared as he let out a long, slow breath, and Hermes cracked his neck. *Here it comes.*

"Where is your caduceus?" Z arched a brow, looking none too pleased.

"Funny story." He let out a nervous laugh. How in Hades' realm was he going to talk his way out of this one? "It seems Pan is in town for the festivities."

Z's jaw clenched, the tendons in his neck bulging as he ground his teeth. "I should have known. This has trickster written all over it."

"Why would you give your caduceus to Pan?" Artemis asked.

"I didn't," Hermes grumbled. "He took it."

"Why?" Hera leaned forward. "And how?" Her brow rose in astonishment.

Hermes sighed. "Remember, back in the day, when I borrowed his panpipes, and he got his knickers in a knot about the whole ordeal?"

"If I remember correctly," Zeus said, "you hid them in a rather unsavory spot."

"Well, he swore revenge, and he got it." He lifted one shoulder in a dismissive shrug. Yes, he was still acting like a moping teenager, but he couldn't help it. He'd been bested by a goat god and betrayed by the woman he loved all in the same act of thievery.

"How did he do it? I ask again," Hera said.

Hermes closed his eyes for a long blink. He really did not want to say this. Yes, Kat had betrayed him, but he didn't want to see her struck down. If he hadn't opened his big mouth and given Hades the details of his excursion to the gates of hell with her, no one would even know she was involved. Now, with all eleven gazes glued to him, he didn't have a choice. "He used the courier," he mumbled.

Hades arched a brow. "The one you had a hard-on for?"

"That would be her."

"I have to hand it to Pan," Hades let out a dry chuckle, "that was quite a feat. I can't believe he pulled it off."

Sadly, I can. He'd put his heart before his head. A rookie mistake.

"This would be one for the record books if the mortals still gave a flying flip about any of us," Hera said as the gods joked amongst themselves about how Hermes had been duped. He should have stayed in bed.

"Okay, okay." Zeus cut his gaze toward Hades' glowering eyes before looking at Hermes. "We all agree this is a historic moment, but Hermes, son, you have got to get it back."

"I know. I'll work on finding him." The band of satyrs from the club last night might be a good place to start. It would take cunning to get them to reveal their ruler's location, but Hermes was the cleverest of the gods. He could pull it off.

"And I meant what I said about your mortal."

"As did I," Hades added, as if Z's threat wasn't enough to kick Hermes' thoughts into a tailspin.

"This was Pan's doing. There's no need to harm the mortal." He cringed as he said the last word. Kat was so much more to him than that. True, she'd ripped a gaping hole in his heart, but death as a punishment didn't fit her crimes. A lifetime of heartache, maybe. No, that was too harsh as well. Perhaps he could gift her with a seven-year stretch of bad luck.

Z rubbed the tips of his fingers together as if creating an electric charge. "It's been a while since I've zapped a mortal."

"Don't kill her," Hades chided, and Hermes almost let out a breath of relief until his uncle continued, "It's been eons since I've dragged one of the living down to hell. Their screams are so… satisfying."

"Please." Hermes scooted to the edge of his seat, stopping short of dropping to his knees and begging. "I doubt she knew what she was getting herself into. I'll fix it. Just, please…spare her."

Zeus narrowed his eyes, his gaze boring into Hermes like he was looking into his soul. His brow rose, and he blinked twice before giving a curt nod. "Get your caduceus back by the end of the day, and your mortal will go free. Fail, and I'll let Hades feed her to Cerberus."

Hermes straightened his spine. *That mangey little chihuahua better keep his chops away from Kat, or so help me…* "Deal."

"Do you have any idea where Pan is staying?" Z rested his elbows on his knees.

"My guess would be out in the swamp somewhere. I can't imagine the god of the wild staying in a hotel."

"New Orleans is surrounded by swampland." Hera leaned back and crossed her legs. "Can you narrow it down a bit?"

"I'll see if I can track down the local satyrs. If they won't spill their boss's location, I'll have to search it all." Which would take forever, even for the god of speed, but what else could he do?

"But right now, he's not in the swamp, is he?" Athena nodded to the television. "He's out there putting people to sleep."

"Not anymore." Poseidon pointed. "Look."

On screen, police were moving the crowds out of the streets, putting a stop to the parade, and dispersing the masses. "Everyone is being sent back to their homes and hotels," the reporter said. "Parades for the rest of the day have been canceled until authorities can figure out what's happening."

Hermes sank in his chair and rubbed his temples. This wasn't a joke anymore. Aside from Kat's life being on the line, Pan was causing mass panic. Typical. That was where the word came from.

"My parade was supposed to happen this afternoon." Poseidon crossed his arms and pouted. "Thanks a lot, Hermes." Leave it to an Olympian to be more concerned about a damn parade in his honor than a life or death situation.

Hermes raised his hands. "I'll fix this. With the crowd dispersed, I'm sure Pan has returned to wherever he's hiding in the swamp. I'll go look for him."

"Even with your speed, it could take days to find a trickster like Pan," Athena said. "You need a better battle plan."

"I can help." Artemis raised her hand. "I'm good at tracking. If we both look, we can find him."

Hermes scoffed. "Thanks, but I don't need help. I've got this."

"What about the courier?" Hades asked. "If she's working for Pan, she probably knows where he is."

Hermes groaned. He couldn't face the woman who'd both bruised his pride and broken his heart. He'd save her life by finding his caduceus, and then he'd be done with her. "I can't."

"Yes, you can." Zeus rose to his feet, crossing his arms and flexing his biceps in a show of power. "You can, and you will if you want her to see tomorrow. Go to her, use whatever means necessary to find out where Pan is hiding, and get that caduceus back." The air in the room grew electric, the way it always did when Zeus was about to summon lightning.

There was no arguing with him now. Hermes would have to talk to Kat.

"Okay, okay." He stood. "I'm on my way."

Kat awoke, slowly opening her eyes and focusing on the ceiling. She lay still, gathering her thoughts and attempting to get her bearings, but she had no idea where she was. The last thing she remembered was Peter, the smelly satyr, taking the caduceus and hitting her on the head.

She groaned, her temples pounding, her back feeling bruised as she lay on the thin mattress. She'd been knocked out by Hermes' staff three times now. This must've been what it felt like when no one caught her before she hit the ground. She needed to have words with Deirdre about her choice in men. Sure, it was Nick's friend who did it, but having friends like that didn't say much about his character.

"Morning, sunshine," a male said before hooves clomped on the wooden floor. "How's your head?"

Kat sat up, squeezing her eyes shut as the room spun. When she opened them, she found a satyr standing by the bed. He wore jeans over his goat legs, and his upper body was bare, revealing a light sprinkling of ginger hair across his pale chest. His horns barely protruded from his curly hair, which meant he was maybe thirty years old—the equivalent of a teen for his species—and hopefully inexperienced.

Kat could take him, but first she needed to figure out what else she might be up against. "Where am I?" She swung her legs over the side of the bed, resting her feet on the floor.

"You're in my house." The satyr sat down next to her. "My name's Jake." He offered his hand to shake, but Kat scooted away.

"What am I doing here?"

"You're being held captive in the game." Jake looked at her like she was crazy...like it was something she was supposed to already know. "Pan said to keep you here until he's done taunting Hermes."

"Pan?" Kat scratched her head and winced when she hit a bruise. "As in the god Pan?" Why on earth would Pan be taunting Hermes? A few days ago, she'd have dismissed the satyr's claim as total BS, but now that she knew the Olympians were in New Orleans, the god of the wild being here too didn't seem so far-fetched.

"There's our Sleeping Beauty." Another satyr came

into the room, carrying a tray. "I made you some oatmeal." He grinned and set it on a table by the bed. "I'm Giorgio."

This guy had umber skin, dark brown eyes, and his horns weren't much longer than Jake's. If the great god Pan thought two juvenile satyrs could hold her prisoner, he was sorely mistaken. Surely a deity wouldn't be so dumb.

Peter was probably sitting in the living room. His thick horns coiled like a ram's, which meant he'd been around the block a time or two…hundred. That might throw a wrench into her escape plan, whenever she figured out what the plan would be.

She leaned to the side, gazing out the open bedroom door. "Pan set the three of you up to kidnap me?"

Jake looked at Giorgio and shrugged. "Three? It's just us two."

"Are you sure? I thought I heard Peter in there, but—"

Giorgio snort-laughed. "She said butt."

"That's what she said." They both guffawed at their ridiculous joke, and Kat rolled her eyes. Perhaps teen wasn't the right age to compare them to. These guys' sense of humor was on par with a twelve-year-old's.

"Why am I here?"

"I told you, you're here until Pan is done taunting Hermes." Jake looked at his friend. "She doesn't listen too well, does she?"

"No, she doesn't." Giorgio scratched his ass before plopping into a chair in the corner of the room.

Fantastic. She was being held captive by the Beavis and Butt-Head of supernaturals. "Why is he taunting Hermes?"

"Are you gonna eat that?" Giorgio pointed to the oatmeal. "Pan said to keep you fed. He'll be pissed if you don't eat."

"Maybe." Kat gave him a pointed look. "First, I want answers."

He pursed his lips, cutting his gaze toward Beavis…er…Jake before focusing on her again. "They have this feud, you see. Hermes started it when he stole Pan's pipes, and now Pan is getting even…with interest." The satyrs looked at each other and laughed like idiots.

Kat scratched her head. It sort of made sense. A little. Both Peter and Nick knew about her plan to take the caduceus, so they must have told Pan what she was up to. Hell, Peter was the one who talked her into stealing the damn thing in the first place.

Holy hairballs. She'd been set up. How could she

be so dense that she let a satyr, of all people, best her? She knew better.

"Peter followed me to Hermes' house last night, didn't he?"

The guys stopped laughing and looked at her. "Who's Peter?"

"The older satyr. The smelly one with big horns." She made a spiraling motion near the sides of her head.

Jake's faced scrunched like he was utterly confused. "You mean Pan?"

"Pan always smells like ass." Giorgio snickered, leaning back and crossing his arms over his bare chest.

"Like swamp ass." Jake snorted again before his face turned serious. "Don't tell him we said that."

"It's not like he'd care." Giorgio chewed on a fingernail. "He gets on us for taking too many showers. I tried to tell him you can't walk around smelling like ass if you live among civilization, but he doesn't get it. Gods are weird."

Weird indeed. Kat bit the inside of her cheek as the realization sank in. Peter *was* Pan. Peter Pan. Just like all the Olympians went by fake names…well, all but Hermes…Pan had chosen a pseudonym as well. A ridiculous one.

She was an idiot. How could she be in the presence of gods and not even realize it? First Hermes and Hades, and now Pan. She hadn't had the slightest inkling of their power. Some badass cat shifter she was. Her emotions had gotten in the way of her common sense, and look where that landed her.

"I get that he took the caduceus to get even with Hermes, but why are you holding me? He got what he wanted. Why not let me go?"

Giorgio leaned forward, resting his elbows on his knees. "You're the interest. Taking the caduceus would have been getting even, but Pan's grudge has grown so much over the eons, he thought Hermes deserved to lose more. So he stole you too. Genius, isn't it?" He scratched his pit before straightening.

Kat closed her eyes and blew out a breath. This was what she got for getting involved with a god. She'd like to say she should have known better, but thinking before acting wasn't her strong point. Neither was her choice in men. Falling for Hermes was her first mistake; opening her big mouth in front of Pan was a close second.

If there was one thing she remembered learning about the gods in school—aside from their overactive libidos—it was that gods were always up to no good. They were selfish, controlling, and they expected everyone to bow down to them.

She was nothing more than a pawn in their game. She had ignored Dad's Rule Number Four and gotten her emotions mixed up in her job. Now she'd lost the caduceus; Hermes would never forgive her after she helped his enemy in their feud, and she was being held captive by Beavis and Butt-Head.

Oh, but it would not end this way. If she could steal from the god of thieves, she could steal from an overgrown satyr easily. Sure, he possessed the strength and stamina of a god, but Kat had the cunning of a woman raised by a thief. She just had to find him.

She picked up the bowl of oatmeal and spooned some into her mouth. It was bland, no cinnamon or honey to give it flavor, which was typical. Satyrs were half goat, after all. They probably ate their oats dry.

"Where's Pan now?" she asked.

"Oh, he's out causing panic," Beavis said as he moved from the bed to sit in another chair.

"And how long are you supposed to keep me here?" She shoved another bite of oatmeal into her mouth and swallowed the sticky substance before setting the bowl on the table. She could play along with their little game until she formulated her plan of escape.

Then, she'd turn the tables on both the trickster gods and get the caduceus for herself.

CHAPTER TEN

A quick Internet search was all it took to find Kat's address. Mortals valued their privacy so much, yet in reality, they had none. They never had. The gods had ways of getting whatever information they needed, and things had only gotten easier as mortal technology progressed.

Sadly, finding the location of the god of the wild wasn't nearly as easy as finding Kat. The Internet didn't provide up-to-date information on gods no one believed in.

With the shelter-in-place order issued for New Orleans, the streets were deserted, the city eerily quiet. Hermes strode down the middle of Royal Street, the same path he'd taken days ago to see the Fates for their enigmatic advice.

He knew better than to infer anything from the sisters' riddles. He should have pressed them for details, but he didn't. Now, he was paying the price. He'd brought the Olympians here for a vacation, but this trip had turned out to be anything but fun.

Fuming with anger—which said a lot because Hermes rarely got mad—he ruminated on what Pan had done. The goat god hadn't just bested him at his own game, he'd made a fool of him. No doubt Pan had chosen Kat, not just for her thievery skill, but because he knew Hermes wouldn't be able to resist her charms. She was everything he'd ever wanted in a woman…and nothing he needed.

It was time Nice Guy Hermes took a hike, and he started acting like the Olympian he was. He refused to be the butt of anyone else's joke, and he would never again fall victim to a mortal woman's wiles.

He slowed his pace as he reached Kat's building, a three-story Creole townhouse, painted beige with green shutters. Her apartment occupied half of the top floor, where a gallery trimmed in wrought iron overlooked the street. A staircase stretched up the side of the building, and a potted fern adorned the third-floor landing.

Straightening his spine, Hermes ascended the steps. He unclenched his jaw and lifted a hand to knock, but he hesitated. He had to push the pain she'd caused him aside and focus on the seriousness of the issue. Once he got his caduceus back, he could return home to lick his wounds, but he would not… under any circumstances…let her see how much she'd hurt him. He rapped on the door.

"Who's there?" a woman asked.

He cleared his throat. "It's Hermes."

"It's about time you brought her home. The door's unlocked. Please close it as soon as you step inside."

Hermes twisted the knob and crossed the threshold, closing the door behind him like he'd been asked. A lamp in the living room and a light from the kitchen provided the only illumination in the apartment. All of the heavy curtains were drawn shut, blocking out the natural light from the sun.

As he stepped farther into the apartment, Kat's roommate, Deirdre, appeared from a darker room. She wore jeans with a lime green sweater, and her smile revealed a set of fangs.

"I thought vampires slept during daylight hours," he said.

"Not *all* the daylight hours. What kind of life would that be? It's one o'clock in the afternoon, and I've been asleep since sunrise. That's plenty of rest." She glanced behind him into the living room and then cast her gaze toward the kitchen. "Where's Kat?"

"I was hoping you could tell me."

She rested a hand on her hip. "She left the club with you last night, and I haven't seen her since. I assumed she was sheltering in place with you." Worry tightened her eyes. "What did you do to her?"

His hands clenched into fists at the irony of her question. "I did nothing to her. It's what she did to me that's the issue right now. Do you know where I can find her? Her life may be in danger."

Deirdre pressed her lips into a thin line and swallowed hard before letting out a nervous laugh. "Have you, uh... Have you tried looking in the underworld?"

"Why would she be in the underworld?"

She gestured for him to follow her to the living room and sank onto the sofa. "She took your caduceus, didn't she?"

Hermes lowered into a chair. "How did you know about that?"

Resting her hands on her knees, she tapped her fingers against her legs before taking a deep breath and looking at him. "Her sister died about a year ago, and Kat feels really guilty about it. She was planning to borrow your staff so she could get down to Elysium and see her…to give her a locket."

"She didn't *borrow* it," he growled. Kat knew how he felt about her. If she needed something delivered to her sister in the underworld, all she would've had to do was ask. He'd have done anything for her. "She stole it…for Pan."

Deirdre shook her head. "She definitely took it so she could get into the underworld, and she was planning to return it as soon as she came back. She never mentioned anything about Pan."

He pulled the crumpled piece of paper from his pocket and shoved it toward her. "Explain this, then."

She took the page, tilting her head and chewing her bottom lip until her brows shot up in realization. "Panpipes."

"Precisely."

Deirdre's eyes narrowed, the tendons in her neck protruding as she clenched her jaw. "No," she muttered. "No, no, no. This can't be." She handed the paper back to Hermes and shot to her feet. "Nick! Get your furry little ass in here. Now."

Hermes twisted in his seat toward the kitchen as a satyr shuffled into the room. Nick's gaze was cast downward, his shoulders slumped, and he wrung his hands, hesitating in the doorway. "Yes, love?" He lifted his gaze to Deirdre then glanced at Hermes and swallowed hard. If *oh shit* were a facial expression, this would be it.

Hermes rose and strode toward the cowering satyr. "Where is Pan?"

"More importantly…" Deirdre stepped beside him and crossed her arms. "Where is Kat?"

"Probably with Pan," Hermes said, "because she's working for him."

"She is not working for him." Deirdre arched a brow at her boyfriend. "Is she?"

Nick's eyes widened as he cut his gaze between Deirdre and Hermes.

"You've bragged about working for Pan since I met you, so I know you know what's going on. Spill it, goat boy," she said. "What have you done?"

"I…I…" Nick stammered. "I didn't do anything. It wasn't me."

"Who was it then?" she asked. "Peter? He egged her on when I tried to talk her out of it."

"His name isn't really Peter." Nick shuffled into the living room, defeated, his hooves scraping across the floor before he plopped onto the couch. "It's Pan."

Deirdre scoffed. "Pan calls himself Peter? Like Peter Pan?" She rolled her eyes. "How original."

"It's his favorite alias." Hermes strode into the

living room and stood in front of Nick. "He thinks it's hilarious."

Nick shrugged. "It is clever."

"I'd expect better from a god," Deirdre said.

Hermes eyed Nick and crossed his arms. Maybe in a show of power. Maybe not. Hey, if he wanted to act like the rest of the Olympians, he had to flex sometimes. And if what Deirdre said was true, and Kat wasn't working for Pan, she might have a third god threatening her life.

His first order of business would be to free her from the goat god's clutches. Yes, she'd hurt him. Yes, he was angry enough with her—and with himself— that he'd just as soon never look into her deep brown eyes again, but he couldn't leave her at the mercy of the horniest, orgy-throwingest deity to ever grace Earth with his presence.

Once she was safe, he'd get his caduceus back, and *then* he'd decide if cursing her with a few years of bad luck was sufficient punishment for breaking his heart. "You had best start from the beginning and tell me what's going on, satyr."

Nick clamped his mouth shut and gave his head a tiny shake.

Okay, now Hermes really did flex. "Unless you

want to face my wrath." He paused for dramatic emphasis. "And the wrath of Zeus."

Nick whimpered before the words tumbled from his mouth, "When Pan heard about Kat's plan to borrow the caduceus, he used the opportunity to get even with you. He egged her on and suggested she use the staff to knock you out if you caught her."

Deirdre gasped. "She knocked him out?"

Hermes' jaw ticked. Zeus would be none too pleased to discover Pan had revealed a god's weakness to a mortal. Of course, if Hermes told, that would add fuel to the fire Z already wanted to burn Kat with, so he'd best keep his mouth shut. "The sphere on the end renders anyone it touches unconscious. She tapped me with it. Continue."

The satyr closed his eyes for a long blink. "Pan stole the staff from Kat after she stole it from you. He's holding her hostage to mess with you."

Deirdre squared her gaze on Nick. "I can't believe you've been lying to me all this time."

His shoulders drew up toward his ears. "I'm sorry, Dee. I didn't want to deceive you, but I didn't have a choice. You can't tell a god no, especially Pan."

She blew out a breath, fuming with anger. "You knew about his plan all along. You knew he was going to use Kat, and you didn't say a word to me. She's my best friend!"

"I'm sorry, babe. I really am, but like I said, you can't defy a god. Ask him." He gestured to Hermes.

He raised his brow. "He's not wrong."

Deirdre's mouth dropped open. "Now you're on his side?

"Oh, no," Hermes said. "I'm on my own side. And now, Nick is too."

"Oh man," the satyr grumbled.

"Oh man, indeed. I assume Pan was at the club where your band played last night?"

Nick sank in his seat. "He was hiding backstage so you wouldn't see him. He followed you when you left."

"I figured as much. He most likely waited for her to finish her..." He nearly said seduction, but he caught the word in his throat before he could humiliate himself anymore. "For her to leave my house with the staff in hand. Where is he keeping her?" He shot a pointed look at the trembling satyr.

"In an apartment a few blocks away."

Hermes hauled Nick up by the arm. "You will take me there now."

"He'll murder me if I do," Nick said. "Worse. He'll make me go insane."

"What do you think I will do if you don't take me there?"

He bleated like a goat. "Okay, I'll take you."

"I'm coming too," Deirdre insisted.

Hermes shook his head. "It's daylight."

"Dammit. Well, tell her to call me as soon as you find her."

"I will." Hermes followed Nick toward the door.

"And you." Deirdre jabbed a finger at her boyfriend. "Don't come back."

"Babe…" He held out his arms to her, but she lifted her chin defiantly.

"I've been looking for a reason to get rid of you, and you just gave it to me. We're done."

"But…" He dropped his arms at his sides.

"Move along, goat boy. Go get my friend back."

Kat eyed the head of iceberg lettuce sitting on the table by the bed. A freaking head of iceberg lettuce. That was the lunch Beavis and Butt-Head provided for her.

Satyrs, of course, were vegetarians, so she expected a meat-free meal. A real salad with some tomatoes and dressing would've been nice. Even a carrot would've hit the spot more than a head of lettuce. It was ninety-six percent water for crying out loud! Then again, at least they fed her *something*. They could have let her starve. Beggars couldn't be choosers, and she was famished, so she picked it up and peeled off a leaf, folding it and shoving it into her mouth. Yum. *Not.*

The television blared from the other side of the closed and locked door—she'd already tried the knob—with the same zombie-hunting video game that Nick and Peter…no, Pan…were playing the day they duped her. What was it with satyrs and zombies?

She polished off her vegan meal, her inner feline protesting the entire time. What she would have given for a good rotisserie chicken right about now. Oh, or some crab cakes with remoulade sauce. *Mmm…*

They'd left her a bottle of water, and while her lettuce lunch was mostly H_2O, she understood the importance of staying hydrated. So she twisted off the cap and chugged the contents. Her last swallow went awry, however, and she inhaled a bunch of water, causing a coughing fit to ensue. As she gasped for breath, the door swung open, and Giorgio, a.k.a. Butt-Head, rushed in.

"Are you okay?" He slapped her on the back as if

she were actually choking on food. "Pan will kill us if we kill you."

She waved away his help. "I'm fine. It's best not to inhale while swallowing."

"That's what she said." He laughed like a moron, and Kat rolled her eyes.

As he got up to leave, she put a hand on his arm. "Hey. Have you heard from Pan? Do you know how much longer I'll have to stay here?"

Butt-Head glanced at the open door, where the sounds of Beavis murdering zombies drifted through. "They shut down the parade, so he headed back to the swamp to recharge his batteries and formulate another plan."

Now there was a piece of information she didn't think she'd get from these idiots. Maybe she could press them for more. "Is he staying in the swamp? Why doesn't he stay in a hotel?"

Giorgio shrugged. "He's the god of the wild. He gets antsy when he's around civilization for too long." He tried to leave again, but Kat held tight to his arm.

"I have to get back to my game. If Jake hasn't killed my avatar already," he pouted.

Up until now, Kat had kept her feminine wiles reeled in. Satyrs were notoriously horny, and she wasn't in the mood to fight off the advances of a couple of teenage equivalents. But sometimes a girl had to do what a girl had to do.

She stroked his arm and turned on the charm. "Wouldn't you rather stay and talk with me?" Batting her lashes, she pulled her bottom lip between her teeth seductively.

Butt-Head's brows shot up in surprise before he regained his composure and squared his shoulders. "Do you want me to stay in here with you, sweetheart?"

Kat's skin crawled, but she managed to grin. "I sure do."

He let out a nervous laugh. "Should I…close the door?"

She licked her lips. "I think you should. We wouldn't want to disturb your friend."

Butt-Head shot to his hooves and crossed the room in two long strides, twisting the knob and quietly closing the door. Then he turned to her, a big shit-eating grin occupying his face. "What now?"

Kat patted the space on the bed next to her. "Tell me more about Pan. I hear he throws some wild parties. Have you ever been to one?"

With a goofy laugh, he plopped down next to her, so close his knee brushed hers. *Ew.*

"Not yet, but he promised Jake and I could come to the next one if we do a good job with you."

"Oh, how exciting for you. Where is the party going to be?" She twirled her hair around her finger. "Maybe I can join you."

His grin widened, and he placed his hand on her thigh. Kat tensed, instinct urging her to push him away, but she didn't. She almost had all the information she needed.

"He found an abandoned shack on the outskirts of the nature preserve. It's the perfect place to hold a party because humans aren't allowed in the park after dark."

Bingo! She knew exactly the area he was talking about. It was time to enact her escape plan. "Would you mind if I use the restroom before we go any further?" she asked with a slight purr. "I haven't been all day."

"Oh, yeah. Absolutely." He stood and took her hand, guiding her out of the bedroom. His palm was clammy, and she fought the urge to recoil from his touch.

As they reached the living room, Beavis hit pause on the game and jerked his head toward them. "What gives, man? She's not supposed to leave the room."

"She has to pee. I could give her your oatmeal bowl if you want."

Beavis huffed. "Fine, but take her right back when she's done. We don't need any trouble."

"You're not the boss of me." Butt-Head puffed out his chest, obviously trying to show off in front of her. If she wasn't so focused on her escape plan, she might have laughed at his performance.

She spotted her phone sitting on a small table by the wall, so she swiped it, tucking it into her pocket before touching Butt-Head's shoulder and drawing him from his ridiculous argument. "The restroom?"

"Right there, sweetheart." He gestured to the right.

"I'll just be a minute." Kat padded through the door and closed it behind her, turning the lock on the knob. The place smelled like a men's room, complete with a dirty toilet and mold in the shower. She wrinkled her nose and pulled back the curtain.

"Oh, this is too easy." First her phone lay in plain sight, and now…the bathroom had a window.

The lock had been painted shut long ago, but she managed to pry it open with a little brute force. As she slid the pane up, it stuck on a pair of screws protruding from the frame. They had been painted in as well, and she didn't have time or a screwdriver to pry them out. Lucky for Kat, her calico would just fit through the crack.

She turned the faucet on full blast to cover up any noises she might make and shifted into her feline form. A pained mewl escaped her throat as the awful sensation racked her body, and she froze. Her heart pounded in her chest as she listened for sounds of the satyrs, but all she heard over the streaming water was the gunfire and groaning zombies of their video game.

She let out a relieved breath and hopped onto the windowsill before slinking out into the daylight.

CHAPTER ELEVEN

"It's 1B." Nick gestured toward a maroon two-story building. "I did what you asked. See ya." He turned to bolt as if he thought he could actually run away from the god of speed.

Hermes reached out an arm—he didn't even have to move his feet, the satyr was so slow—and grabbed him by the back of his shirt, dragging him toward the door. "Knock."

"Aw, c'mon, your godliness. You won't hurt your knuckles if you do it."

"Don't press your luck." He tightened his grip, a low growl rumbling in his chest. This creature was lucky Hermes was the one dealing with him. If he'd mouthed off to Hades—or, hell, *any* of the other gods—he'd be a smear on the pavement by now. "I know satyrs. Your friends have a secret knock, and you're going to tap it out."

"Yes, sir." Nick's voice rose an octave. He hesitated when he lifted his hand, but then he pounded out the "Shave and a Haircut" rhythm.

Hermes pursed his lips. Kat was right about that pattern being too easy. He'd have to convince Hades to change it if they wanted to keep the underworld free from thrill-seekers. Medusa would have a field day with guys like this.

A couple walked by on the sidewalk behind them, their gazes bouncing from Hermes' face to his fist knotted in the back of Nick's shirt. The woman opened her mouth to speak, but Hermes inclined his chin, his godly presence intimidating enough that she changed her mind and scurried along. He hated scaring mortals like that, but he didn't have time to defuse a confrontation with words.

"Who's there?" a trembling voice called from the other side of the door.

"It's Nick. Let me in, dude."

"What's the password?"

Nick ground his teeth and cut his gaze to Hermes, whispering, "Pan threatened us with our sanity if we told the password to anyone but a satyr."

"And I'll castrate you if you don't say it now," he

whispered back. "It'll be hard to participate in the orgy I'm sure he's planning if you don't have balls."

Nick cleared his throat and leaned toward the door, mumbling.

"I couldn't hear you," the man inside said.

"Aphrodite sucked my cock." He flinched as if he expected to get smacked for uttering such blasphemy.

Hermes laughed. "You must have a death wish. Don't expect the god of the wild to come to your aid when Addie finds out your secret phrase."

"You're not gonna tell her, are you?" Nick whined like a child.

"Oh, I certainly am. It's too good not to."

The door opened a crack, and a man with pale skin and curly ginger hair peeked through. "Is Pan with you?"

Nick hesitated before replying, "No. C'mon, Jake. Let me in."

Jake blew out a relieved breath. "Thank the gods." His relief didn't last long, however. As Hermes shoved Nick through the door, the younger satyr whimpered and backed into a wall.

Hermes stomped through the living room, past another satyr sitting on the couch, and threw open a bedroom door. The space stood empty, so he continued his search, opening every door, searching every closet, but Kat wasn't there. "Where is she?"

"W…w…where is who?" Jake sank onto the couch next to his friend.

"Don't play games with me, boy." Yes, he flexed again. With Kat in trouble, he could out-flex *and* out-glower Hades himself if he had to.

"Seriously, man. He knows everything." Nick joined them on the couch, and they all lowered their heads like schoolboys being scolded by the principal.

"It's Giorgio's fault!" Jake elbowed the satyr in the ribs.

"It is not!" He returned the gesture, hard enough to make Jake shout, "Ow!"

"Silence." As Hermes crossed his arms and flexed yet again, all three satyrs sank further into the couch. No wonder Zeus and Hades did this so much. It actually worked! "I will ask you one more time. Where is Kat?"

"We don't know," Jake grumbled.

"Does Pan have her?"

"I don't think so," Giorgio said.

Hermes' nostrils flared. He was known as the most easy-going god on Olympus, but the satyrs were testing his patience. "You don't want to see what happens when the god of thieves loses his cool, so I suggest you stop messing around and tell me every-thing you know."

Jake shot his friend the stink eye, and Giorgio ground his teeth, the side-to-side motion making him look like a goat chewing cud.

"She disappeared," Giorgio said.

"You mean she escaped," Jake snapped.

"There's no way she escaped." He lifted his hands and dropped them in his lap. "She never left the bath-room, until she was gone."

"How is she gone if she didn't leave the bath-room?" Jake rolled his eyes, shaking his head like he thought his friend was the bigger idiot. Hermes hadn't decided who earned the title yet.

"Like I said, she disappeared. There's no way a human body would fit through that small crack in the window. I don't know what happened."

"This bathroom?" Hermes strode toward the open door.

"It's the only one we've got." Jake followed with Giorgio on his heels, while Nick didn't leave his spot on the couch.

Hermes stepped into the bathroom and threw back the moldy shower curtain to find a small window with a narrow ledge.

I see what you've done, little thief. He chuckled and

slid the window open, but it caught on a set of screws protruding from the frame. The six-inch gap was just enough space for the small calico to slink through.

"See?" Giorgio straightened his spine and smiled proudly. "I told you she wouldn't fit through the window."

"You would be surprised." Hermes peered through the glass at the ground below before turning around. "How long ago did she go missing?"

The satyrs looked at each other, and Jake scratched at the base of his tiny horns. "An hour maybe? An hour and a half?"

"Does Pan know she's gone?"

"We don't have a death wish." Giorgio backed up as Hermes brushed past them and returned to the living room.

"Have you done anything to track her down?"

"No." Jake looked perplexed. "How could *we* find her?"

Hermes rubbed his thumb and forefinger against his beard. It had been less than half an hour since he left Kat's apartment. If she didn't return home immediately after her escape, she probably had another plan. And he'd bet his left nut that plan involved getting his caduceus back.

"Tell me where I can find Pan."

"Don't think about it, man." Nick rose to his hooves and walked toward the others. "The moment you picture it in your mind he'll know how to get there."

Hermes arched a brow. Were these misfits seriously trying to disobey a god? Flexing would only get him so far. There was a reason the Olympians turned to Hermes when they needed assistance, and it wasn't for his brute strength. He could outwit the cleverest of creatures with his eyes closed. "I hear Pan has an orgy planned for tonight."

Both Jake and Giorgio's gazes flicked to him.

"And those swamp nymphs…" He let out a low whistle. "Talk about wild. I wonder where they'll be gathering?"

Giorgio squeezed his eyes shut, his expression pinched as if it pained him not to think about where the party would be. That or he was severely constipated; it was hard to tell. A whimper emanated from Jake's throat a moment before the location of Pan's hiding place flashed in his mind.

"The nature preserve. I should have known." Hermes held out his hand. "Give me your phones."

"Oh, man." Giorgio pulled his phone from his pocket and handed it to Hermes. "That's my lifeline."

"I can't have you tipping off Pan that I'm on my

way, now can I?" Not even the god of speed could get there faster than a phone call could connect. "Hand them over."

Nick gave him his phone. Jake grumbled, but he followed suit and placed the device in Hermes' hand.

"On the couch. All of you." He waited for the trio to plant their goat asses on the sofa before he unplugged their gaming console and tucked it under his arm. "Do you see that clock?" He gestured toward the wall.

The satyrs nodded.

"You will not move your asses from this spot for the next two hours. If you do, I will know." That was a lie. His magic didn't work that way, but these guys didn't know their tails from a toilet plunger at this point. "After that, you're free."

"If you're taking our phones and our games," Jake said, "what are we supposed to do while we sit here?"

Hermes shrugged. "Talk to each other. Have a circle jerk. I don't care." He strode to the door, pausing in the threshold after he opened it. "Maybe you should decide how you're going to avoid Pan's wrath when he discovers you failed him."

All three sets of eyes widened in their sockets as the satyrs paled. Hermes chuckled and closed the door behind him before setting their electronic devices on the ground next to the outside wall, cloaking them in magic so only their owners could see them.

If Pan's minions followed directions and stayed put, Hermes would be in and out of the old goat's shack before they left the living room. If they got a wild hair and decided to press their luck, tipping off Pan before Hermes got there, well…he might have to flex a little more.

"Thanks for the ride." Kat tipped her driver and climbed out of the car in the parking lot of the nature preserve. The Welcome Center was a one-story building with a flagstone façade and a pitched roof with dark brown shingles. She could go inside and pay the entrance fee like a good girl, but at ten bucks a person, she'd pass. She spent the last of her monthly income on the Uber to get here. Besides, she wasn't here to enjoy nature; she was on a mission.

Slipping into a wooded area beside the parking lot, she checked her surroundings for witnesses before shifting into her calico. It was against the law for shifters to enter places like this in animal form. Too many of her kind gaining free admission before returning to human form inside—Kat included—prompted the government to put restrictions on their magic.

Get caught on a first offense, and you'd have to pay a hefty fine. With Kat's criminal record, she'd be sent straight to jail. She'd have to make sure she didn't get caught.

With a flick of her tail, she slunk along the chain-link fence separating the parking area from the preserve. A family with six kids poured out of a blue minivan, and a little girl with shiny black ringlets bounded toward her shouting, "Kitty!"

Kat froze, her back arching and her fur puffing out like a fluffball as a hiss escaped her throat.

The girl stopped, staring at her for a moment with her mouth hanging open before letting out an ear-piercing shriek. Kat didn't mean to scare the little girl, but she couldn't fight her feline instincts. She backed up, lifting a paw with her claws extended, and the girl's mother ran toward her, grabbing her by the arm.

"You leave that cat alone. It probably has rabies." The mother dragged the girl toward the Welcome Center.

Rabies? As if. But Kat didn't have time to take offense. The commotion drew the attention of a park employee, and he strode into the parking lot, his eyes wild with alarm.

Kat darted into the bushes to hide. The man and the family conversed, but Kat couldn't hear what they said. Seemingly satisfied that nothing nefarious went down, he escorted them inside.

Whew. That was a close call. The last thing she needed was to end up behind bars, whether it be a jail cell or one at animal control. She trotted a few more yards away from the building before scaling the fence and taking off into the woods.

Massive oak trees towered over the preserve, their branches dappling the afternoon sunlight filtering through. Kat's paws barely made a sound as she ran across the soft earth. She had no idea where she was going, but she felt pulled toward the east, almost as if by magic…or fate.

Fifteen minutes later, she spotted the rundown shack through the trees. Similar to the old bokor's place, the structure had a slanted front porch and rotting wood. But this place looked like it had never been painted, and gaps between the wooden slats would do nothing to stop the chilly air from seeping inside. You'd think after all these millennia, even the god of the wild would prefer the modern comforts of central heating and running water. Apparently not.

Kat crouched as she approached the building, creeping up on the house with stealth. Well, she thought she was being stealthy. But as she reached the front porch, in a flash of magic, someone grabbed her, hauling her away from her destination. She shrieked, clawing at the culprit and slicing into his neck.

"Ouch!" A single drop of golden ichor dripped from the wound before the skin stitched itself back together, and Hermes clutched her with both hands beneath her front legs, holding her away from his body. Of course it was Hermes. Who else would it be?

"Calm down. I'm not going to hurt you. Though you are a naughty girl who deserves a spanking for what you've done." Mirth danced in his hazel eyes a moment before he scowled. "Or worse."

Oh, you'd like that, wouldn't you? Typical man… wanting to be in control. Though she had to admit, the thought of Hermes bending her over his knee did send a little thrill rushing through her veins. *Don't fall for it, Kat. Gods are selfish pricks, just like thieves.*

"I suppose you were planning to slink inside and take it like you took it from me?"

She growled low in her throat, and Hermes sighed. "You aren't familiar with Pan's magic, are you?"

He paused as if he expected her to answer, but she was a cat. All she could do was meow.

"Pan has the power to drive you mad. 'Panic'? 'Pandemonium'? Those words originated with the god of the wild." He cradled her to his chest and kneeled. "I'm going to put you down. Will you please shift to your human form so we can talk? I can't have you getting hurt in a feud between gods."

He set her paws on the ground but hesitated to let her go. "Please don't run from me out of fear. You've broken my heart, but I would never harm you."

Well, damn. She'd planned to bolt the second he released her, but hearing those words from his lips, how could she?

As he let her go, she called on her magic and returned to human form. Her muscles tensed, freezing her in pain and making her double over as the awful skin-crawling sensation did its thing.

"Are you okay?" Hermes clutched her shoulders, his eyes tight with worry. "Did the satyrs harm you?"

"I'm fine." She waved off his assistance and straightened. "And I did not break your heart. I'm nothing more than a pawn in your little game with Pan. You used me."

He tilted his head. "On the contrary. You used *me*."

"I did not."

"I see." He rubbed his beard. "So you didn't sleep with me in order to steal from me?"

"Of course not! How could you even suggest such a thing?" Well, she could see how he would jump to that conclusion, but it wasn't her fault. If dumbass Pan hadn't knocked her out, she'd have been to Elysium and back by now and had the chance to explain why she took it in the first place. Guilt gnawed in her gut, so she turned on her heel, attempting to stomp away, but Hermes caught her by the hand.

"Your anger is misplaced, dearest." He cringed when he said his pet name for her. "Pan is the one who used you. Not me. The only thing I'm guilty of is revealing my feelings to you way too soon in our relationship…but even that wasn't my fault, was it?"

She sucked in a sharp breath and spun around, ready to argue, but what could she say? He was right…about all of it. Her anger—which was misplaced, just like he said—melted away as she finally met his gaze. "Did you really mean all of that stuff you said when you thought I was a normal cat?"

He released her hand, his jaw clenching as he spoke, "Every word of it, and you used my vulnerability to your advantage."

Her throat thickened, the pain in his eyes telling her it was true. Hell, she could feel it in her bones. Hermes was the man of her dreams, and she had deceived him. Gods, she was an idiot. "I'm sorry, Hermes. I don't know what I was thinking, but I promise I did not sleep with you just so I could steal from you. I really do care about you."

He lifted his hand to silence her. "Save it. I'm going to take you home, and then I will return to claim what's mine from the old billy goat."

"Let me help you. It's the least I can do." *Now that I've utterly ruined any chance I ever had with you.*

"I don't need assistance."

"Hey." She cupped his cheek in her hand, and he stiffened before leaning away, out of her reach. "Will you at least let me explain what happened?"

Sighing heavily, he crossed his arms over his chest. "I don't have time to listen to your excuses." His expression pinched, and he dropped his arms at his sides. "I have to retrieve my staff by the end of the day. Your life depends on it."

"My life?"

"Indeed. Both Zeus and Hades have placed a target on your back after the trouble you and Pan have caused."

It wouldn't be the first time someone wanted her

dead. In her line of work—her *old* line of work—she'd found herself in plenty of pickles. Though, if two gods wanted to take her out, she didn't stand a chance. "All the more reason for me to help you, then."

"Kathryn, I don't—"

She crossed her arms. "Pan didn't just steal from you. He stole from me too…and it's my life that's on the line. *We* are going to get the caduceus back. End of story." And maybe she could make it up to him in the process.

CHAPTER TWELVE

Despite his better judgment, Hermes wanted to smile. Damn, she was hot when she was bossy. Perhaps he should give her a spanking for what she'd done. One last romp between the sheets before he bid her goodbye forever wouldn't hurt, would it? He gritted his teeth. *Focus on the issue at hand.*

He didn't require her help, but she was right about one thing. Pan had wronged them both…and her life hung in the balance. Okay, make that two things she was right about. He could let her tag along for the ride. "We'll need a plan. Pan isn't going to let the caduceus go easily…if he even still has it in his possession."

"Why wouldn't he have it? Isn't that the point of your game? To take each other's stuff?"

"The fun is in the taking, not the keeping. Much like when you stole the young man's watch and wallet but immediately returned them. Pan has had his fun with my staff. He doesn't need it anymore."

Kat leaned her back against a tree, worry tightening her eyes. "I hope Agnes and Vern are okay. Does Pan know they're alive? What if he's not feeding them?" She tilted her head. "Do they need to eat?"

"They spoke to you?"

She nodded.

His heart thrummed. The snakes never spoke to anyone but him. Well, aside from their hissing matches with Medusa's hair, but that didn't count. If they'd broken character in front of Kat, perhaps she did play a more important role in his life than stealing from him.

"No need to worry about them. They're magical snakes. They don't need food, though they do enjoy a bite of steak every now and then." He chuckled. "It makes them feel like pythons. I don't enjoy cleaning the mess that comes out when they're done, so it's a rare treat."

"They poop?"

"Everyone poops."

Kat nodded as if he'd just answered a question that had been burning in her mind.

The ease of their conversation made his heart ache. He wanted to stay angry with her—to hate her, even—but her concern for Agnes and Vern gave him pause. Maybe he could spare a few minutes for her to explain herself before he saved her life and was done with her. He eyed the locket hanging around her neck. "Tell me something, Kathryn."

"Anything."

As she held his gaze, he pressed his lips together, studying her before he spoke, "What is so important about that necklace that you would betray me just to take it to your sister in a realm no living mortal should ever venture inside? I assure you Elysium is a pleasant place to spend eternity. She is at peace."

"I'm not." Sadness filled her eyes as she lowered her gaze and opened the locket. "It holds a picture of our mother and me. If she'd had it with her when she died, it would be with her spirit form in Elysium."

He shook his head, his brow furrowing. "You knew how I felt about you. Why didn't you simply ask me to take it to her? Why the deception? Why lead me on?"

"I didn't lead…" She sighed. "The day Camilla died, I had taken her to the doctor for some tests. She left her locket in the car because she was having scans done, and she didn't want to lose it. When we got home, it was pouring, and she forgot it was in the console. I put her to bed that evening, and she begged me to get the necklace for her. I said some things I shouldn't have. Things *no one* should say. Terrible, awful…"

Kat shook her head as if chasing away the memory. "She went to sleep, and she never woke up."

He pulled her to his chest and held her tight as she sobbed.

"I just want to tell her I'm sorry."

Aaaand…there went his heart, melting like chocolate in a fondue pot over an open flame. Guilt and regret must've pressed heavy on her shoulders because she slumped into him, and he was happy to carry the weight for her. He didn't know if he could trust her, but one thing was for certain. He loved her, whether she felt anything for him or not.

"Help me retrieve my caduceus, and I will take the locket to your sister. I'll tell her of your woes and return with her forgiveness for you. How does that sound?"

She inhaled deeply, lifting her head to look into his eyes. "Like something I should have asked you to do in the first place. Does this mean I'm forgiven?"

He wiped a tear from her cheek. "I've never found myself in this position before, and I'm not sure how I want to handle it. Let's take it one step at a time, shall we?"

She nodded and pulled from his embrace. "We'll get your staff back. Wait… You said Pan had his fun with it. What did he do?"

"I guess your captors didn't allow you to watch the news. He ran through Mardi Gras, tapping people with the ball and putting them to sleep in masses. The festivities have been canceled until further notice, and a shelter in place has been ordered in the French Quarter."

Kat gaped. "Mardi Gras has been canceled?"

"Indeed."

"Oh, that's just awful. Do you know how much money the carnival season brings in for the city? Businesses have ordered tons of extra product. Thousands of pounds of food will go to waste. They'll never recover from the financial blow if we don't fix this, Hermes. People will lose their jobs. Their homes."

He rested his hands on her shoulders. Normally, he wouldn't concern himself with mortal affairs, but the passion and concern in her voice moved him. He would fix this for her. "One crisis at a time, dearest. My first order of business is retrieving my caduceus. Then I'll worry about saving Mardi Gras."

"You mean *our* first order of business. You better

not try to trick me. If you whisk me home and do this by yourself, I'll never forgive you."

He arched a brow. He wasn't sure he'd forgiven her, but… "We can't have that, can we?"

"Where do you think he's hiding your staff? Maybe you can distract him while I slip in and take it."

Good question. "When I stole his panpipes, I left them in a pile of manticore dung in the middle of a vast grassland."

"Manticore—" Kat gaped. "Why would you do that?"

Hermes shrugged. "It was a joke. He told me to eat shit when I called him an old billy goat, so it seemed like the logical place to hide his pipes."

Her lip curled. "That's nasty."

"Perhaps I went too far?"

"Ya think?" She paced a few steps past him, peering through the trees. "Where are we? I can't see the house anymore."

"Far enough away that he won't know we're here until we're ready."

"What are we going to do? Walk in and ask him where it is? Will he tell you?"

"Not without some coercion. We'll have to catch him first. Hold him hostage like he did to you and threaten him with something that would devastate him."

Casting her gaze upward into the canopy, Kat chewed the inside of her cheek, looking thoughtful and ever so adorable. "I have an idea. Can you get some rope?"

"Mortal rope won't hold a god, but I know something that will." Artemis, the huntress goddess, had an arsenal of divine weapons, including an enchanted rope that could hold the mightiest of Olympians. "Wait here."

"Oh, no you don't." Kat clutched his arm. "You are not ditching me, mister. We're in this together, remember? Where's your bike? Wherever you're going, I'm going with you."

"It would take you half an hour to walk to it, dearest."

"Then you'd better give me a piggyback ride."

Feisty and determined. Now if she only meant it when she said she cared about him. There was one way to find out. "Have I told you what an intriguing woman you are, Kathryn of NOGS?"

Rather than letting her answer, he took her face in his hands and kissed her. She slid her arms around him and melted into his embrace like she belonged there. *Sweet sirens,* the desire she returned was enough to incinerate him right there in the swamp. That kind of passion couldn't be faked, could it? Gods, he hoped not.

He broke the kiss, grinning, and he winked before turning his back to her. "Hop on. I'll try not to go too fast for you."

Clutching his shoulders, she jumped and wrapped her legs around his waist. "Don't hold back on my account. I can handle it."

"We'll see about that." He sprinted through the trees.

Kat gasped, wrapping her arms around his shoulders and holding him in the biggest bear hug he'd ever received. He weaved through the trees at the fastest speed a mortal could survive, reaching his bike in two minutes flat, which unfortunately didn't give him enough time to enjoy the feel of her breath against his ear.

As her feet slid to the ground, he held her and then turned around. "Are you all right, dearest?"

Her knees wobbled a bit, but the light in her smile rivaled a thousand torches on Mount Olympus. "That was amazing."

He chuckled and tossed her a helmet. "You haven't seen anything yet."

They mounted his Ducati and arrived at the

rental house five minutes later. He parked three houses down to avoid announcing his presence to the other Olympians. "Does your plan require anything other than rope?"

She rested her chin on his shoulder, keeping her arms wrapped tightly around him, and he relished the affection…maybe a little too much. She had squashed his heart, after all. Should he be so quick to forgive? If he were going to behave like a true Olympian, that answer would be a resounding *hell no*.

"Just the big cypress tree in front of the shack." She gave him a squeeze before releasing her hold and sliding off the bike.

"Are you planning to snare the god of the wild?" He set his helmet on the seat.

"Do you have a better idea?"

"I don't. It's genius. I do have one question, though. What will we use as bait?"

She smiled. "You, of course. With a peace offering to draw him out."

"I love the way your mind works. I know just the thing, but you will need to wait here. I don't have time to explain to Zeus why the woman who stole my staff is now helping me retrieve it. Plus, right now, he wants you dead, so…"

"All right. Make it fast." She kissed him on the cheek.

"Always." With a burst of godly speed, he darted into the backyard and scaled the same lattice Kat had used the night before. Inside his room, he tiptoed to the door, cracking it to listen for signs of the gods.

Clash of the Titans played on the television downstairs, one of the Olympians' favorites. They would all be glued to the screen for the next hour, so Hermes slipped out the door and snuck down the hall to Artemis's room. It didn't take long to rifle through her things and find the enchanted rope and the peace offering. The gods really should be more careful with their magical artifacts. They were way too easy to steal.

Then again, Hermes wasn't one to talk anymore, was he? He chuckled at himself and ducked into Hera's room to grab a few supplies, tucking them into a satchel before slipping it over his shoulder. Without a sound, he exited through the balcony door and returned to his bike, where he found a pretty little calico sitting atop the seat.

Kat flicked her tail before shifting to human form, groaning as her body shuddered. She cracked her neck and shook her arms. "A police cruiser is casing the neighborhood. I didn't want to get busted for violating the shelter in place order."

"Is shifting painful?" He put the stolen items into the side pannier and strapped his helmet to his head.

She climbed onto the bike behind him. "It's because I'm half-human. Happens every time. I'm used to it."

When this ordeal was over, he'd have to find a way to help her with that. They sped back to the nature preserve and parked behind a tree alongside the highway. Hermes cloaked his bike to hide it from curious eyes and took Kat's hand as they walked into the woods.

"I will keep you safe. If Pan so much as flicks a grain of sand in your direction, he will wish he was never born."

Kat stopped and rested her hand on his cheek. "I never doubted that you would. We make a good team."

His breath caught, but he kept his expression neutral. He'd have to contemplate his relationship with Kat later. If she didn't live to see tomorrow, there would be nothing to ponder. "Ready for your piggyback?"

"Hell yeah, I am!" She hopped onto his back, and they dashed through the forest. He went a little slower this time, allowing himself a moment to enjoy the feel of her body against his before stopping a few yards away from Pan's hideout.

"Do you think you can get him to come out near that tree?" She pointed to one in front of the house.

"I'm sure I can, but can you lay the trap without him hearing?"

She scoffed. "I stole from the god of thieves. What do you think?"

He arched a brow.

"Too soon? Yeah…" She put her hands on her hips. "I'm a trained cat burglar. I can do it. Besides, Beavis and Butt-Head told me he came here to recharge his batteries. I assume a god who parties all night sleeps all day, right? And he spent the morning wreaking havoc in the French Quarter, so he's probably out cold."

Hermes couldn't hide his smile if he wanted to. She was ingenious, perceptive, and insanely gorgeous on top of it all. It was no wonder he'd fallen for her faster than Medusa could turn a man to stone. "I'll do a quick run by the windows to peek inside and make sure. Here's the rope."

"Okay. If he's not…"

Before she could finish her sentence, he zipped

around the structure and returned to stand in front of her. "You were right. He's snoring like a Minotaur with a head cold."

Kat's mouth hung open for a second before she snapped it shut. "Okay. My turn."

Hermes stepped back and watched her work. She made a loop with a slipknot at one end of the rope and tossed the other over a thick bough in the tree. Then she bent some branches, creating a spring-like mechanism and turning the rope into a snare. *Impressive.*

When she finished, she dusted off her palms and moved to stand next to him. "My part's done. Your turn."

Hermes inspected her contraption. The structure was ingenious. So good, in fact, he couldn't have done it better himself. "Where did you learn this skill?"

"My sister's dad was a hunter. Before he left my mom, he taught me a few things." She shrugged, her face taking on a disgusted look before she continued, "If I need to catch my dinner, I'd just assume hunt as my calico."

"You have a hard time trusting men."

"Whatever gave you that idea?" She smirked.

"You can trust me."

"I know. Now, go do your thing. I'll be hiding up a tree, so I don't get caught in the crossfire if things get ugly."

He nodded once, and Kat transformed into her calico before climbing a nearby trunk.

From the safety of her perch on the highest branch she dared climb to, Kat watched as Hermes approached her snare, positioning the loop—which was buried in dead leaves and twigs—between himself and the decrepit front porch.

"Pan," he called, his voice booming with confidence. "This ends now. Return my caduceus and I will forgive your transgressions." He searched the trees until his gaze landed on her, and he winked.

Her stomach fluttered at the gesture, but she forced her emotions aside for the time being. She might have to pray to Eros for help winning Hermes' heart later. She wouldn't blame him if he never wanted to see her again after this, but she planned to do everything within her power to prove herself to him. Now, she was about to see the gods in action. Stretching out on the branch, she laid her head on her front paws and waited. And waited.

After a few minutes, when Pan didn't appear, Hermes raised his voice even louder. "Come on out, brother. I'm here bearing gifts."

A thud sounded from inside the shack, followed by hooves clomping across the wooden floor. The front door swung open, and the stinky old goat god sauntered onto the porch like he was the king of the swamp.

Good gravy. She could smell him all the way up in the tree. What was Deirdre thinking letting someone with body odor that bad sit on their couch? He'd probably blown mind dust in her face the moment he stepped through the door, because Deirdre was a stickler for scents, what with her enhanced vampire senses and all.

Kat fought the urge to growl. If they were doing this one hundred percent her way, she'd pounce and claw Pan's eyes out for what he'd done. Though, based on how quickly Hermes healed when she scratched him, she wouldn't make it past the first swipe of her paw before Big Billy Goat Gruff overpowered her. It was best to let Hermes handle this part of the plan.

"The god of thieves has met his match." Pan walked down the rotting front steps and crossed his arms, stopping a few feet in front of the snare. "Admit

I'm better at stealing than you, and I *might* return what's yours."

Hermes' laugh sounded way too cocky. "Never."

Oh, come on. If that's all Pan wants, let go of your pride and say it. You don't have to mean it. Jeez! The Percy Jackson series wasn't too far off in its depiction of the gods and their egos. Had he forgotten her life was in danger?

"It wasn't you who bested me anyway," Hermes gloated. "It was a mortal."

"Which makes your situation even more pathetic." Pan smoothed his matted hair away from his face. "Will you smite her?"

Hermes' nostrils flared. "I would never harm her. She's my… I'm her patron god. If anything, I'm impressed by her skill, and she will be rewarded for her wit."

Rewarded? She could think of quite a few ways Hermes could reward her. *Purrr…*

Pan scrunched his face before rolling his eyes like he was bored with the exchange. "You won't find her."

"I already have."

The goat god forced a hard breath through his nose. "You were always too clever for your own good…unlike my satyr followers, it seems. What gift have you brought for me?"

Hermes reached into his bag and pulled out a dagger. Solid gold from tip to pommel, it glinted in the afternoon sun. "Artemis's knife. You never cared for her hunting in your forests. Return my caduceus, and I'll keep my mouth shut, let her think you stole it yourself."

Pan's jaw moved from side to side like he was chewing. "Bring it here. Let me verify it's really hers."

Hermes took a step back. "You come here. I won't fall victim to your tricks this time."

"There's no trick." Pan huffed and dropped his arms at his sides. "Fine." He walked toward Hermes, and Kat held her breath. His first step into the snare didn't trigger the release. *Crap!* Had she done something wrong?

He paused, his gaze locked on Artemis's knife, and he licked his lips. *Come on, goat man. One more step…*

"I can return it to her if you're not interested." Hermes opened the top of his satchel and moved the knife toward it.

"No! I want it!" Pan lunged, his hoof hitting the loop of rope and activating the snare. The bent branch swung upward, pulling the rope with it, and the slipknot tightened around Pan's ankle. Wait… Did goats have ankles? Anyway, it cinched around his leg right above the hoof and yanked him from the ground.

He hung upside down, bouncing like an over-stuffed piñata at an eight-year-old's birthday party, and Kat stifled her meow-laugh.

"How dare you! Let me down!" Pan's face turned red from either his position or anger…she couldn't tell which.

Hermes held up the knife, examining the blade, touching his finger to the tip as if he were actually considering using it. *Holy hellhounds.* He wasn't going to gut the goat, was he? He said this was a game. Surely torture wasn't in his repertoire of moves.

He pointed the tip toward Pan's face. "Where is my caduceus?"

"I'll never tell."

He rested the blade on Pan's hairy cheek. "Don't make me use this."

Hermes, no! Kat rose to her paws, ready to jump down and stop him. This was not the man she knew. Hermes was kind, fun-loving, and smart. He wasn't a sadist. He couldn't be.

When Pan clamped his mouth shut, Hermes slid the blade from his chin up to his earlobe, shaving off his gnarly facial hair in one even stroke.

"Not my beard!" Pan struggled, but Hermes grabbed his shoulder, holding him still.

"I've always wondered how well you'd clean up. Let's find out."

He shaved the other side of Pan's face, leaving nothing but a long, grizzly goatee, and Kat let out a breath. *This* was her Hermes, torturing the god of the wild by giving him a makeover. She was tempted to shift back to human form and make a video, but she thought better of it. Hermes probably wouldn't appreciate going viral on social media.

"It's just hair." Pan feigned indifference. "It'll grow back."

"I wonder how long it will take?" Hermes clutched the long tuft on his chin and severed it with the blade, holding it up so Pan could see. "That's got to be at least twelve inches. In your human form, here on Earth, I'd say it'll take a year for it to return to its former glory."

His face reddened even more. "Laugh all you want, herald. I still have your staff."

"Okay. Welcome to *Ambush Makeover,* Olympian style." In a flurry of godly speed, Hermes used the blade to finish shaving Pan's face and give him a nice haircut. Sheared short on the sides and back, with two inches of wavy locks left on top, his hair looked presentable, if not…nice. Pan did clean up well. He wasn't the most attractive man Kat had ever seen—Hermes would always hold that title—but he looked decent enough. He still stunk to high heaven though.

"You can say uncle anytime." Hermes tugged a hand mirror from his bag and showed Pan his reflection.

The goat god bleated. He actually made goat noises, even though his upper half looked human. "You'll rue the day you were born when I'm free."

Hermes laughed. "I highly doubt that. Are you ready to talk?"

"No."

He let out a dramatic sigh. "I didn't want to do this to you, old friend, but you've left me no choice." He rummaged through his bag and pulled out a pale blue aerosol can.

Kat squinted, creeping forward to read the words scrawled across the aluminum. Was that deodorant? His secret weapon for getting Pan to return the caduceus was a can of Degree? What was he going to do? Spritz him to death?

"What is that?" Panic flashed in Pan's eyes for the first time.

"It's called deodorant. All the mortals use it these

days… Well, the ones who socialize with others do. You should try it." Hermes gave Pan's shoulder a shove, spinning him and spraying the deodorant across his body.

"No!" Pan squealed and bleated again. "Baaa! Not my manly musk. Not my alluring aroma. You've ruined me!"

"All you have to do is return my caduceus. Just say when." Hermes shoved him again and stepped back, fanning the cloud from his face as he continued spraying.

"How will I seduce the ladies? My mojo is gone, you imbecile. It's taken me centuries to perfect my amorous odor."

Hermes shook the can, whistling like he didn't have a care in the world, and continued his assault.

"Okay, okay! I'll talk. I'll tell you where to find it; just let me down and stop with the rancid stench bomb."

If he thought the deodorant smelled bad, he needed to take a whiff of his own pit. *Jeez!*

"That's a wise decision, old friend. Next up was Hera's perfume."

"Blasphemy!" he shouted as Hermes released the snare, letting Pan drop to the ground with a *thunk*.

"Nonsense. It smells like wild roses." He lifted the

pink bottle to his nose and took a sniff. "It's quite nice."

Pan sat upright, rubbing the base of his horns and glaring at Hermes.

If Kat's calico could smile, she would have been grinning to the tips of her whiskers. She supposed, being an immortal, you'd have to find ways to make your existence a pleasant one. And Hermes chose tricks and games rather than meddling in mortals' lives. She could get on board with his form of fun.

"Well?" Hermes wound up the rope but left the loop wrapped tightly around Pan's goat ankle.

"I don't have it," he grumbled, fidgeting with the knot. When he couldn't loosen it, he threw his hands in the air, frustrated. "I hid it for safekeeping."

Hermes nodded. "I figured as much. Tell me its location, and I'll be on my way." He continued winding the rope around his hand and elbow until it pulled taut on Pan's hoof.

"Someone is watching it for me. A fellow wilderness dweller. Good luck retrieving it."

Hermes pulled the rope, dragging the two-hundred-pound goat across the dirt as if he were light as a down pillow. "Is it here in Louisiana?"

"In this very swamp. He worships a different set of deities, but he's quite the character. I wonder if he knows how close he lives to the underworld." He gestured to the loop around his ankle. "May I?"

Kat couldn't stop the low growl emanating from her throat as Hermes released him. She knew exactly whom Pan left the caduceus with, and retrieving it would be the hardest part of the game.

CHAPTER THIRTEEN

"I don't know a lot about voodoo," Kat said as she walked by Hermes' side across the soft, damp ground. "But I do know that man is pure evil. The religion itself is not, but he takes his powers to the extreme." They'd dropped the bag containing Artemis and Hera's things into his bike's side pannier and were headed down the familiar path to the bokor's cottage.

"Not to worry. Unless the man is a deity himself, his magic will have no effect on me." He held her shoulders and looked into her dark eyes with his smoldering gaze, attempting to put her fears at ease while simultaneously trying to ignore the war waging between his head and his heart. "I've got this."

"Do you really?" Her wary expression said she

wasn't the slightest bit convinced. "I'm not sure Pan is done with his tricks."

"It will be fine. I promise." In fact, he hoped Pan had another trick up his sleeve. Otherwise, retrieving his staff would be far too easy. He needed the distraction to help his subconscious sort through his emotions because, right now, he felt like he was at the tippy top of a rollercoaster track, ready to plunge either into the ride of his life or the pits of hell, and Kat could take him to either place. "You wait here; I'll get the caduceus, and then we'll talk."

"Be careful please." She pressed her lips to his. Her kiss was sweet as honey, and the emotion she put into the gesture told him her apprehension was sincere. When was the last time anyone expressed concern for his safety? He thought back as far as his memory would go. His mother had been worried when he snuck out of his crib to steal Apollo's cattle shortly after his birth. Aside from then, he couldn't recall another time.

"I'll be in and out before you know it." Caution had never been a dominant trait for Hermes, and there was no need to start now. The bokor may have been powerful, but he was a mere mortal. Nothing Hermes couldn't handle.

"I'll be right here waiting." Kat crossed her arms and leaned against a tree.

"I won't keep you long." He winked and zipped through the forest to the old man's shack.

Hermes scoffed as he approached the dilapidated building. If he were really so powerful, surely he could afford better accommodations. Whether through magically enhancing the structure or selling his services to the mortals, he could at least clean up the peeling paint and make the building structurally sound.

To say Hermes was unimpressed was an understatement. The man was nothing more than a hermit, and rumors had turned into tall tales until he became feared. He jogged up the front steps and knocked on the door. The slant of the porch created a funhouse effect, and Hermes shook his head to chase away the dizzying sensation.

The door swung open, and the grizzly old troll scowled up at him. "Who dares trespass on my land?"

He chuckled. If he hadn't seen this guy before, he'd have assumed this was part of the game. Sadly, the bokor really thought he lived in a grim fairytale, so Hermes got into character. "It is I, Hermes, god of thieves. I've come to claim what's mine."

"What's yours?" The man squinted as if he couldn't see well.

"Yes, what's mine."

The bokor shook his head. "No. What *is* yours? I have no idea what you're talking about."

He huffed. Was this guy for real? "You have my caduceus. Pan told you to hold on to it. Does that ring a bell?"

"The stick with the golden snakes?"

"That would be the one."

"Right, right. Come in." The man shuffled inside, and Hermes followed.

Kat sat with her butt in the dirt and her back against a tree, waiting for Hermes to return. She had a bad feeling about this, and not just about her chances at proving to him her feelings were sincere. No one ventured into this part of the swamp unless they were desperate or had a death wish. The bokor practiced illegal magic. Curses, hexes, and raising the dead were just the beginning of the services he offered, and the price he required was often more than the customer could pay. And she didn't mean money, either.

But Hermes was a god, for goodness' sake; she

didn't need to worry about his safety. He could probably zip in and out of the shack before the bokor even knew what happened. Except…if he'd zipped in, he'd have been back in a zap. What was he up to?

A sinking sensation formed in her stomach. The bokor's magic might not affect Hermes, but a god's would. From her own experience, she knew damn well that a mortal could wield a godly instrument. She'd knocked Hermes out cold with his own caduceus. What if the bokor did the same?

The sinking turned into a hollow feeling deep in her core. What if the old man put Hermes to sleep and then used some other artifact against him? Pan could have given him a weapon along with the staff.

"You didn't think about that, did you, mister?" The god of luck's fortune may have just run out. "Dammit, Hermes." She'd been sitting here for half an hour. He'd have been back by now if nothing had gone wrong.

Which meant something *had* gone wrong.

Kat shifted into her calico and trotted through the forest, cursing the sexy, carefree god the entire way. She paused when the house came into view, her heart sprinting in her chest. Never in her life could she have imagined she'd confront a black magic man, but here she was, about to do just that.

She prowled toward the porch but made a sharp left at the steps and went around to a side window. It didn't have a ledge to perch on, but the soft wood gave against her claws, allowing her to hoist herself up the wall to look inside.

The small structure contained two rooms: a combination living/kitchen area and a bedroom. Though calling it a kitchen was a stretch. His amenities consisted of a wooden table with a propane-powered camping stove, a tea kettle, and a wicked array of knives. *Yikes.*

The bokor sat in a chair, flipping through the pages of a heavy book. The caduceus lay on an end table, but Hermes was nowhere in sight.

Kat released her hold of the rotting wood and slunk around to the back of the house. The view through this window showed her the bedroom: a mattress on the floor and a lamp. Jeez, this guy was a minimalist.

Where was Hermes? Her stomach sank again. *Please tell me he's not buried out here in the swamp.* This was supposed to be a game he played with Pan, but the bokor could have changed the rules.

Oh, Hermes. Your cockiness has gotten you into trouble, hasn't it?

Hoping to find an open window, she prowled

around the perimeter. She'd gotten lucky at Beavis and Butt-Head's place with an easy escape. She shouldn't have expected the same here. All the windows were shut tight. The doors too. It was time to put her acting skills to the test with the old injured feline routine.

If her heart beat any faster, it might explode, but she climbed the front steps and assumed the position anyway. Lying on her side, she let out a pained screech and followed it up with a mewl that could raise the dead from Hades' hands. She moaned, letting the deep sound reverberate through her body before letting out another screech.

Footsteps stomped across the floor, and the door swung open. "What the devil? I'm trying to read." The bokor's perturbed expression softened into an evil grin. "I haven't had cat for dinner in ages. Come here, kitty, kitty."

Oh, crap. She'd hoped to play on his humanity for an injured animal, not to become his next meal. Scrambling to her feet, she darted through the open door.

The bokor followed her inside, snatching a cleaver from his blade collection as he chased her toward the table. Kat shot beneath the ratty sofa, backing up against the wall, out of his reach.

"Come on out, you mangy little bitch." He kneeled on the floor and peered beneath the couch.

Oh, no you did not. No one called Kat a bitch. Okay. What were her options here? The two-foot-long caduceus was way too big for her to drag out in her feline form, so she had to shift. She growled low in her throat, racking her brain for another option. The moment she transformed, the bokor would probably whack her with a curse, turning her into a slug. But she had no other choice.

The man swiped the knife beneath the sofa, narrowly missing Kat's front paw. She screeched and scurried to the corner of the couch, slipping out from under it and calling on her magic to transform.

As she shifted to human, she snatched the caduceus from the table a moment before her body seized from the change. She groaned, unable to move for a second, which was all the time the bokor needed to understand what was happening.

He gasped. "A shifter. I should have known." He hurled the cleaver toward her, and it clipped her shoulder before *thunking* against the wall and falling to the floor.

"Ouch!" Sharp pain shot through her deltoid, and blood dripped down her arm. She looked left and right, trying to formulate an escape, but she was cornered.

"Pan said he'd be working alone, but I knew better." He lifted his hands in front of his body, and energy shimmered between his palms.

Holy hairballs. She was in trouble now. Kat lunged over the table, swinging the caduceus toward him as she tumbled to the ground. Sadly, she missed her target, and the impact caused the staff to slip from her grip. It slid across the wooden floor, stopping beneath the blade collection. Even worse, the impact also felt like it shattered her elbow where bone met wood. *Fantastic.*

Her shoulder throbbed, and her elbow screamed in pain. She was certain it was broken, and though it would heal on its own, thanks to her shifter magic, her human side would slow the process. If she were a purebred, she'd already be good as new. Instead, her left arm was out of commission for the time being. Good thing she was right-handed.

"I don't need Pan's help to curse you, sweetheart. How would you like to spend eternity as a mouse?"

She let out a pained laugh. "Is that the best you can do?"

"Are you questioning my power?" The energy

between his palms crackled, turning red with his magic.

Whoops. She knew better than to taunt a black magic man. Hermes was rubbing off on her. Kat used her right arm to drag herself to a sitting position, and her stomach lurched. Add a concussion to her list of injuries. How hard did she hit the floor? If she could just grab the caduceus, she could get out of this situation. The staff or one of the knives, she didn't care which at this point.

"Here, kitty, kitty." The bokor gave his power one more pulse and hurled it toward her.

Kat rolled quickly—thanks to her cat-like reflexes—and the magic struck the floor, exploding in a ball of fire. Damn, was he going to turn her into a mouse or incinerate her? She didn't plan on sticking around long enough to find out. She scrambled to her feet, but the bokor lunged, wrapping his arms around her legs and sending her toppling to the floor again.

This time, she caught herself before she could smack wood. She reached out for the staff, but it lay a foot away from her fingers.

"A little help here, guys?" she ground out, trying to kick free from the bokor's grasp, but he was unnaturally strong for a decrepit old fart.

At her request, the snakes came to life. They

uncoiled from the staff, though their tails remained attached to the handle, and they dragged the caduceus across the floor, inch-worm style, until Kat could reach it.

Her legs were pinned beneath the bokor's body, and as he held up a hand, gathering energy in his palm again, Kat swung the staff, knocking him in the head with the sleepy ball. He collapsed on top of her, snoring like a congested bear, and she wiggled herself free.

"Thanks for the help, Agnes, Vern. I thought I was toasted catnip there for a second."

"Thank you for asssking," Agnes hissed.

"It's niccce to feel needed," Vern added.

Kat rose to her feet and peered down at the old man. "How long will he be out?"

"The sphere grantsss a solid eight hours," Vern said.

She rotated her shoulder, flexing and contracting her bicep as her cut healed and the bone mended. *Ahh… That's better.* "Has Hermes been here? Do you know what happened to him?"

"He's in that box over there." Agnes gestured with her head to a wicker basket sitting on the floor in the corner.

The container was half the size of a litterbox.

There was no way Hermes would fit in there. Kat swallowed hard. "Is he okay?"

Agnes laughed. "Go see for yourself."

She picked up the box and set it on the table next to the camping stove, laying the caduceus next to it. Gripping the lid, she leaned away and cringed as if the thing might explode in her face when she opened it. Or worse. It could contain Hermes' severed head, but that was a path she refused to let her thoughts venture down. She'd seen *Se7en*. This scene wasn't about to become a horror movie. As she opened the lid and peeked inside, she found a small green turtle staring back at her.

"Hermes?" She cocked her head.

The turtle blinked.

Kat looked at the snakes. "Is that him?"

"In the shell…er…flesh," Agnes snickered.

"Pan gave the bokor a jar of transformation dussst." Vern slithered up the side of the box and looked inside. "When Hermes waltzed in like he was invincible, the old troll blasted him with the dust and turned him into a turtle."

"I've tried to warn him hisss ego could be as big as Zeus's, but he wouldn't lisssten." Agnes re-coiled herself around the staff. "So now the god of ssspeed is one of the slowest creaturesss on earth."

Fighting her smile, Kat scooped Hermes into her hands and held him up near her face. He looked into her eyes briefly before lowering his little turtle head, ashamed.

She laughed. "Oh, Hermes. What am I going to do with you?"

Blink, blink was his only reply. Did turtles even make sounds? She'd have to Google it later.

"Is there a way to reverse the spell?"

"Only Pan can undo the magic." Vern returned to his position on the caduceus. "You'll have to bring him an offering."

Kat cringed. "About that… I don't think Pan is going to be up for doing Hermes any favors after what he just did."

CHAPTER FOURTEEN

"I seriously can't believe I'm doing this." Kat grabbed a magazine from the rack and lowered her head, her ears burning as she made her way to the cash register. The periodical was encased in black plastic with only the title scrawled across the front in bold white letters: *Babes with Boulders.* "Are you sure a bowl of oatmeal wouldn't be good enough?" *Jeez Louise.*

"You have to bring out the big gunsss if you want to win over Pan." Agnes slithered on Kat's wrist as she spoke, tickling her. "The raunchier, the better."

She'd had to walk back to the Welcome Center at the nature preserve, where she called an Uber to pick her up. The snakes assured her Hermes would repay her for whatever expenses she incurred to get him back to his normal form, so she dipped into her meager rainy-day fund to pay for the ride and the erotic magazine she was about to purchase.

Vern had suggested she take Hermes' bike into town, but she'd experienced that thing's speed. If she tried to drive it, she'd end up dead in a ditch within the first mile.

She shuffled forward in the checkout line, and when it was her turn, she laid the magazine on the counter face-down. The cashier arched a brow, a slow smile spreading across his face as he looked at her and then at her purchase.

"Is this for you, or is it a gift for someone else?"

Kat crossed her arms. "Would you ask a man the same question?"

"Umm… No, I was just curious." He picked up the magazine and scanned the barcode.

"They say curiosity killed the cat, but that expression works both ways."

He swallowed hard. "Six-fifty, please."

She waved her phone over the little machine on the counter, draining her meager savings even more. *This had better work.*

With her purchase tucked under her arm—and Hermes tucked in her pocket—she strode onto the sidewalk and called for yet another rideshare. Her account would be empty by the time she finished this little adventure.

As she traipsed across the soggy ground toward Pan's hideout, she found the god of the wild soaking in a muddy offshoot from the bayou. He sat immersed up to his chest—she hoped to Hades he wasn't naked beneath—playing a slow, sad tune on his pipes. He didn't seem to notice her approach, so she cleared her throat.

He set his instrument on the ground and spoke without turning around. "Ah, Kathryn. I see you've outsmarted my minions. I'm impressed."

"It wasn't very hard." She inched closer to him. Muddy swamp water wouldn't be anyone's first choice for a bath, but considering the way this old goat reeked—before Hermes doused him in deodorant— he probably wasn't trying to get clean.

"I suppose I should have left you with some more experienced satyrs." He turned toward her and held out his hand. "Come join me."

Her lip curled. "In the mud pit?"

"It's not all mud. See?" He scooped the water into his hands and let it drip back into the swamp.

It was dark brown and thick as blood, and the smell…rotting foliage, animal dung, stagnant water. *Gross.* As a shifter, Kat's sense of smell was far better than the average mortal's, which, in this case, was not a good thing.

"I'd rather not." She tugged Hermes from her pocket, holding his tiny turtle body in her palm. "Will you please change Hermes back to his human form? I brought you an offering." She lifted the bag containing the magazine.

Pan laughed. "I'll consider your request if you join me."

Kat's nostrils flared as she fought the disgusted expression trying to distort her face. *You better remember this, Hermes.* She kicked off her shoes and waded into the murky water. Mud squished between her toes as she sank down, her butt meeting the shallow bottom when the water reached her shoulders.

"What have you got for me?" Pan made a grabby motion with his hands.

She offered him the magazine and lowered her arm into the water, holding Hermes in her palm just above the surface.

Pan unwrapped the plastic, laying it on the ground behind him, and flipped through the magazine, nodding in appreciation. "Someone has done her homework. Erotic images are my favorite. Though, I don't know why they insist on including articles in these things. No one reads them." He gingerly set the magazine on top of the discarded plastic.

Kat glanced at the bracelet on her wrist, but the snakes had returned to their golden form. Hermes wasn't kidding when he said they only spoke around him. Well, him and her now. "I found an excellent source for information."

"Indeed you did. I accept your offering, under one condition."

She held in a groan. Hopefully he didn't expect her to attend his next orgy. If so, Hermes would have to get used to carrying his house around on his back because he'd be a turtle forever. Just the thought of what the grimy old goat probably *wasn't* wearing beneath the water made her stomach sour.

"When I turn Hermes back to his human form, I want him to admit—out loud—that I bested him. That I am the better trickster god, and he lost the game."

Oh jeez. She stood corrected. He had a better chance of getting her to attend an orgy than to get Hermes to admit the goat god was better than him. Pride was one thing gods did not lack. "Do you mind if I have a word with him?"

"Be my guest."

Kat rose to her feet and waded a few yards farther into the swamp. Hopefully there weren't any hungry gators around looking for their next meal. She wasn't in the mood to wrestle with a reptile.

"Hermes," she whispered, "you have got to do what he says. I have no idea how to change you back otherwise."

The turtle blew a hard breath through his nostrils and pulled his head back inside his shell.

"Now you listen to me, mister. This game has got to end now. I have a job to do, and if I don't earn my paycheck, I won't be able to pay my bills. I can't spend any more time running around, playing with a god. If you don't do this, I'll have no choice but to take you to Zeus and let him handle it."

Hermes peeked his head out of his shell, slowly extending his neck and gazing up at her. Turtles couldn't really create facial expressions, so she had no idea what he thought about her threat…but she could imagine.

"Do you promise to say what he wants you to say? You don't have to mean it; you just have to say the words."

His head bobbed up and down, which she took as a yes, so she waded back toward Pan and sank down into the water next to him.

"All right, Pan. You win. Hermes agrees to admit you're better than him if you will change him back and end this game now."

Pan grinned, giving Kat a view of his goat teeth. Bits of grass and seeds were stuck between them, and a dark yellow film covered his enamel. *Yuck.* Hermes should've threatened him with a toothbrush to begin with.

"This has been fun, old friend." Pan flicked his wrist toward the turtle, and Hermes transformed back into his human self, standing waist-deep in the swamp.

He started toward Pan, but Kat grasped his arm, tugging him to her side. "Tell him what he wants to hear," she said through clenched teeth.

Hermes grunted, glancing at her before returning his gaze to the other god. "You win, Pan. What can I say? You're better than me."

Pan smiled smugly. "Words I never thought I'd hear from you."

Hermes shook his head and climbed onto the bank, offering his hand to Kat to pull her out. She rose to her feet, dripping wet with mud, muck, and stench, and she shook her legs, sending clumps of swamp rot raining to the ground.

"I'm hosting a party tomorrow night," Pan said. "You are both welcome to attend."

Hermes straightened his spine and chuckled. "You should be aware, old friend. Zeus knows about your little escapade with my caduceus. If I were you, I would hightail it out of here before he found me."

Pan's eyes widened, and he swallowed hard. "Thanks for the tip. I'm glad we're parting on good terms."

"Good terms indeed," Hermes mumbled as he turned and led Kat away from his rival. Why did she get the feeling their game was far from over?

"I cannot believe that old billy goat got the better of me," Hermes growled as he marched through the woods toward his bike, dragging Kat along behind him. Hermes was older, more experienced. He was the god of thieves for Zeus's sake.

"I'm losing my touch, being forced to live on Earth. Perhaps it's time I hang up my wings." Gods knew he didn't need them anymore. Zeus had essentially rendered them all useless the moment he shut down Olympus. Sure, they still had their magic, but his whole *don't intercede in mortal affairs* rule made Hermes feel almost impotent.

And Pan had turned him into a gods-damned turtle, for fuck's sake!

Kat gave his hand a squeeze. "The only reason he was able to do it was because he stole it from *me*. And the only reason I was able to steal it from you was because I took advantage of our relationship. If you're going to be upset with someone, it should be me."

"Hmph. I suppose you're right about that." He continued his march through the woods. He *should* have been upset with her. He should have been livid, but as he stomped over the mossy earth, Kat nearly jogging to match his pace, his mind joined forces with his heart, dissolving what was left of his doubt.

"I'm so sorry, Hermes," she said. "I was stupid; I acted without thinking, and I'm sorry I hurt you. I wish there was some way I could make it up to you."

Hadn't she already? She'd faced one of her biggest fears and battled the Voodoo man to save him. When she had his caduceus in her clutches, she could have easily run away, leaving Hermes behind and traveling to Elysium, but she hadn't. She'd rescued him *and* convinced Pan to lift his transformation spell…which was a feat in itself. The goat god probably would have left Hermes in turtle form for a millennium otherwise.

No, his anger now stemmed solely from wounded pride. No wonder the other gods treated him like a joke. He'd earned it. He would have to come up with a plan to get even with Pan. To prove his worth.

"Some god of thieves I turned out to be." Was he pouting? Sure. Was it something he should have been doing in front of the woman who just saved his ass? Absolutely not, but he couldn't help himself.

"Hey." Kat stopped and tugged his hand, moving in front of him to look into his eyes. "You are still the god of thieves. I can't do anything about you being forced to live on Earth, but I can tell you this… You are a wonderful man with a good heart, and whether you believe it or not, you have stolen mine. That's a feat *only* the god of thieves could accomplish. I love you, Hermes of Olympus, or Seattle, or wherever you happen to reside."

He held her gaze, letting her words seep into his soul. In his entire existence, no one had ever said that to him. His heart swelled with joy, and he tucked her hair behind her ear, trailing the backs of his fingers down her cheek. "And I love you, Kathryn of NOGS, goddess of my heart. But we are not out of the woods yet."

CHAPTER FIFTEEN

"Are you sure about this?" Kat slid off Hermes' bike in the rental house driveway and handed him her helmet.

"You are my soulmate, dearest. They'll have to get used to it." He offered his hand, and she laced her fingers through his.

"If you say so." Her pulse thrummed as they ascended the front steps onto the porch and paused outside the door. She was to blame for everything that went down. If she'd kept her mouth shut and not blabbed, right in front of Pan, about meeting Hermes, none of this would have happened. She could only hope the other Olympians would be as forgiving.

Hermes turned to her, taking her shoulders in his

hands. "We'll have to explain everything that happened, but first we need to get cleaned up. Hera will have a fit if we drip swamp muck all over the furniture."

"I'll follow your lead." She took a deep breath and stepped with him through the door.

As soon as she entered the foyer, a big man with dark hair and a well-defined jawline shot to his feet. With his broad chest and overpowering presence, he could only be Zeus. "What's the meaning of this?" He gestured to Kat.

Hermes tugged her to his side. "Z, guys, this is Kat. She's my soulmate."

A look of astonishment flashed on all their faces before a woman with purple-silver hair and golden eyes rose to her feet and smiled. "It's so nice to meet you, Kat. I am Artemis."

"Oh, hi! Thank you for—"

"We're going to get cleaned up." Hermes pulled her toward the stairs, not letting her finish her thank you. "We'll explain everything later." He held up his wrist, where his caduceus now resided, and Zeus nodded, returning to his seat in the recliner.

Hermes practically dragged her up the steps and into his bedroom before closing the door and setting his bag on the dresser.

"I was trying to tell Artemis thank you for letting us borrow her things. That was very kind of her."

"She didn't exactly agree to it." He took the items from the bag and said, "I'll be right back," before zipping down the hall and returning in a blink. "Now she'll be none the wiser." He grinned and gripped Kat's hips, attempting to tug her body to his, but she braced her hands against his chest.

"You didn't ask her, did you?" She stepped away from him. "You just took it."

He held up his hands in a show of innocence. "It's what I do. I'm—"

"Don't give me the god of thieves excuse. Taking things in jest or as part of a game or rivalry is one thing, but her belongings could have been damaged if things had gone differently. What if Pan had put up more of a fight? What if he'd snatched the dagger out of your hand and disappeared before you could catch him?"

He dropped his arms at his sides. "Then Artemis would be without her dagger."

"And it would be *your* fault. I've learned my lesson, but it appears you haven't. Artemis seems like a lovely person. If you'd asked for her help, I'm sure she would have given it to you."

He balked. "Ask for her help? Dearest, if there's

one thing you should know about me, it's that I'm the cleverest of the gods. I require help from no one."

"No one?" She crossed her arms. "I see. So, you escaped the bokor, reclaimed your caduceus, and got Pan to turn you back into your human form all on your own?"

"Of course, I…" He paused and pursed his lips. Casting his gaze upward, he narrowed his eyes as if contemplating her words.

Kat let him ruminate. She could tell him she helped him until her face turned blue, but he wouldn't believe it until he came to the conclusion himself. So she waited, watching the array of emotions cross his face as he thought.

Finally, he looked at her, chewing his bottom lip as the realization dawned in his eyes. "Actually, I couldn't have done it without you. I'd still be a turtle in a box if not for your help. Thank you." He chuckled, shaking his head as he moved toward her, gripping her hips again. This time, she didn't pull away. "I'm afraid you might make me a better man if I'm not careful."

And he might make her a better woman. "It's okay to ask for help every now and then. You don't have to prove your worth to anyone."

"I'll try to remember that." He peeled his shirt

over his head and dropped it on the floor. "I believe I could use your help with one more thing." He kicked off his shoes and stepped out of his remaining clothes.

Holy moly. Would she ever get used to the sight of him? "I would be happy to offer my support. What can I do for you?"

"Would you mind helping me in the shower? I could use some assistance with those hard-to-reach places." His playful smile made her knees feel like jelly.

Trailing her fingers across his shoulders, she stepped behind him and wrapped her arms around his waist. "Just the hard-to-reach places?" She slid her palms down his stomach to grip his dick. "Not the ones easy to get to?"

"Mmm… I need help with *all* the places."

"See?" She glided her fingers up to his chest, trailing kisses along his neck and reveling in the way her touch raised goosebumps on his skin. "That wasn't so hard, was it?"

He chuckled and turned to face her. "Oh, it's very hard, dearest. May I?"

As he reached for the hem of her shirt, she lifted her arms over her head. "Be my guest."

After removing her shirt, he took off his bracelet and paused. "I better put this somewhere for safekeeping. Come." He guided her into the bathroom and set the caduceus in a cabinet beneath the sink.

Then, he kicked the door shut and finished undressing her, tossing her wet clothes aside and stepping back to sweep his gaze up and down her form. "Your beauty truly does rival that of a goddess."

His eyes smoldered as he closed the distance between them, and her stomach fluttered, a thrilling hum cascading through her veins as he slid his fingers into her hair and pulled her mouth to his. He kissed her greedily, possessively, and she leaned into him, holding him tight. She belonged to him, and the thought made her head spin.

With a deep inhale, he pulled away and turned on the shower. Steam wafted from the stream as the water heated, and he held her hand, helping her into the tub before following and closing the curtain.

Kat tipped her head back, letting the warm water soak her hair as Hermes lathered soap between his palms. Then he washed her. He glided his hands along the dips and curves of her body, caressing every inch of skin as if she were the most precious creature he'd ever seen. Judging from the longing in his eyes, perhaps she was.

When she was good and soapy, he moved on to her hair, massaging her scalp with citrusy shampoo before working conditioner through the length of her locks. As she tipped her head back to rinse, he quickly washed himself, his gaze never straying from her eyes.

"It's not every day a cat shifter gets worshipped by a god," she said.

"It will be for you." He crushed his mouth to hers.

His skin was soft, his body hard, and as he leaned into her, pressing her back against the tile, she held him, memorizing the way he felt in her arms.

Right. Everything about Hermes felt right.

He reached for her leg, tugging it upward to his waist and moaning into her mouth. "I need you, Kat."

"Then take me. I'm yours."

He closed his eyes, letting out a long exhale as if her words had reached all the way to his soul. When he opened them again, so much emotion filled them, she nearly choked on a sob. "I love you." He pressed his tip against her.

"I love you too." She gasped as he filled her.

He held still, gazing at her with an awed expression, letting the moment soak in. Hermes really did love her. She felt it all the way to her bones. As they stood there, joined together as one, the rest of the world slipped away.

He moved, sliding in and out of her slowly, the friction sending electricity shooting through her limbs. Holding her gaze, he continued the motion, his rhythm steadily increasing in speed with each thrust of his hips.

"Oh, Kat."

The growly way he said her name did her in. Her orgasm coiled tightly in her core, releasing in an explosion to rival Mount Vesuvius. She tried to be quiet. There were eleven other gods downstairs, and while they probably knew what was happening, they didn't need to know how thoroughly Hermes was rocking her world.

But she couldn't help herself. She cried out, moaning his name, and his entire body shuddered with his release. They stood still for a moment, joined together, his body pressed to hers, her back against the wall, and they just breathed.

She clung to him, an overwhelming feeling of completeness settling in her soul. Hermes felt like home.

He smiled, releasing her and brushing a soft kiss to her lips before shutting off the water. "Zeus will be expecting an explanation. Let's talk to him, and then I'll continue worshipping you, as I plan to do every day from this point forward."

"I like the sound of that." She wrapped a towel around her chest as Hermes returned his bracelet to his wrist and strode into the bedroom.

A soft knock sounded on the door, followed by Artemis's voice. "I have some clothes for Kat."

Hermes put on his pants, and Kat opened the door to take the stack of fabric from the goddess. "Thank you." She motioned for Artemis to enter the room. "Hermes has something he'd like to tell you."

"I do?" He gave her a quizzical look.

"You want to tell her how she helped you get your caduceus back." Her tone sounded way more commanding than she planned, but he was a man. Sometimes they acted like big kids, gods included.

Hermes screwed his lips over to the side, considering her request. "I'm not sure I do." See? A big kid.

"I'm *certain* you do." She set her borrowed clothes on the dresser and crossed her arms, arching a brow.

He cut his gaze between her and Artemis, who stood in the doorway, looking at him expectantly. "All right," he huffed. "Artemis, I borrowed your rope and hunting knife to capture Pan. I returned them when we were done, so no harm, no foul, right?"

Artemis shook her head. "Why am I not surprised?" She looked at Kat. "You've got a big job ahead of you if you're planning to keep this one in line."

Kat pinched Hermes on the cheek. "I'm looking forward to the challenge."

Artemis closed the door behind her, and Kat dressed in her tan cargo pants with a light green sweater. As Hermes finished buttoning his shirt, another knock sounded on the door, more insistent and much louder than Artemis's soft rap.

"Hermes!" Zeus's voice boomed from the hall, and Hermes swung open the door.

"Pack it up. We're heading out." Zeus turned to leave.

"Heading out?" Hermes asked. "We have the house for another week."

Zeus whirled around to face him, irritation pinching his expression. "Have you not been watching the news?"

"I've been a bit busy."

"Mardi Gras has been completely canceled. The mortals are launching an investigation. All magical beings will be questioned, and we aren't sticking around to get involved."

Kat sank onto the edge of the bed and clutched Hermes' hand. "We have to do something."

"This is a mortal problem," Zeus grumbled. "And the gods don't deal in mortal affairs anymore."

She shot to her feet. "But gods *caused* this mortal affair. You're already involved."

Zeus puffed out his chest like a pissed-off gorilla, his nostrils flaring as he exhaled. *Whoops.* Talking back to the king of the gods probably wasn't in her best interest, especially when he'd threatened to kill her once already. But she couldn't let Mardi Gras be ruined. Her friends depended on it for their livelihoods.

"Remember your promise. I got the caduceus back, so her life is spared." Hermes moved to stand between her and Zeus, looking over his shoulder and giving her a wink before turning to the elder God. "She's right. I am partially responsible for the mayhem, so I will stay behind and fix it."

Zeus let out a dramatic sigh. "Normally I would tell you to get your ass on your bike and follow us home, but seeing as how you've chosen a mortal as your mate, I suppose their affairs are now yours. You're on your own."

CHAPTER SIXTEEN

ermes held Kat close to his side, waving at the other gods from the porch as they pulled on to Esplanade and drove away.

For the most part, he agreed with Zeus that the gods shouldn't get involved in mortal affairs. Delphi knew the mortals didn't care about them anymore. But he wasn't lying when he said he felt partially responsible, and he would do anything for the woman by his side.

As they returned to the living room, he dropped onto the couch and patted the cushion next to him. She sank onto the seat and rested her hand on his knee. Damn, it felt good to be with her.

"What if we went to the authorities?" she asked. "We can explain what happened, and then they can return to the festivities, knowing it was a simple prank that won't happen again."

Hermes laughed. "Hades no, dearest. One: Zeus would have my balls mounted to his bike if we informed them of our presence here, much less that we're responsible for the ordeal. Two: I highly doubt anyone would believe us if we tried. The Olympians at Mardi Gras? Most people don't even believe we exist."

"Do you have a better idea, then?"

He tapped his fingers on the arm of the couch as a plan formed in his mind. "We simply need to make them forget it happened."

She raised her brows, surprised. "Do you have that kind of power? I mean, a vampire can glamour an individual, sometimes a small group, but can you glamour the entire city?"

"I can't, but I know something that can. Are you familiar with the river Lethe that runs through the underworld?"

"The one people have to drink from before they can be reincarnated? The one that makes them forget their entire lives?"

He nodded. Someone paid attention in social studies class. "I'm certain I could swipe some without the goddess knowing. The question is, how do we get the entire city to drink it?"

"We want them to forget a single event happened. Not cause widespread amnesia."

Hermes rubbed his beard. She had a point. A single sip from the river was enough to make a person forget they ever existed, and he had no idea the dosage required to make them forget only the past week. One drop, perhaps? Maybe two? "We have a problem then, don't we?"

He rose to his feet and paced in front of the sofa, clutching his hands behind his back. He was loath to admit it, but it seemed he would require another god in order to fix this problem.

"The goddess Lethe has the power we need. I'll go to the underworld and kidnap her. Then we can—"

"Or…" Kat rose and stood in front of him, placing her hands on his shoulders. "You could go to the underworld and *ask* for her help."

He narrowed his eyes. "You don't understand. Being a trickster and a messenger, I constantly have to prove my worth to the other Olympians. No one takes me seriously as it is. If I ask a minor god for help, how will that look?"

"It will look like you're smart enough to ask for help when you need it."

"I don't—"

She rested her hand on his cheek. "The other Olympians ask you for help all the time, right?"

He nodded. What was she getting at?

"Does that make them any less powerful? Does anyone look down on them for needing your assistance?"

"I guess not."

"So why would they look down on you if you ask Lethe for help?"

"I see your point. I've never thought of it that way." He chewed the inside of his cheek, pondering the idea. "It would be clever to ask Lethe for help, just like it was clever of the Olympians to ask for my help in freeing Ares from the giants' prison."

"Exactly. Asking for assistance isn't a sign of weakness; it's cunning."

"You're right." He chuckled. Where had this woman been all his life? "A visit to the underworld is in order. Will you be okay here alone? I promise to make it quick."

"Will you take me with you?" Kat batted her lashes, the hopeful look in her eyes tugging at his heart.

He sighed heavily. He wanted, more than anything, to fulfill this wish for her, but… "There are some rules I simply cannot break, and this one is at the top of the list. No living mortals are allowed in the underworld. I'm so sorry."

She nodded, pulling from his embrace. "I understand."

"Hey." He lifted her chin with his finger. "When this is done, I will take the necklace to your sister and deliver your message. I promise."

"Thank you." She sank onto the couch and straightened her spine. "You best be on your way then. I'll be fine here…as long as Pan doesn't come looking for me."

"I'm sure he's already hightailed it out of town. I'll be back before you know it."

She arched a brow. "That's what you said when you left for the bokor's place."

He laughed. "This time, I mean it."

Hermes pushed his Ducati to its limits, jetting to the swamp and then racing past the bokor's house faster than the old troll could blink. When he arrived at the door to the underworld, he didn't hesitate, tapping his caduceus against the wood and ducking inside.

Steamy heat engulfed him as he traveled down the rocky path and hitched a ride with Charon to cross the river Styx.

He made his way toward his destination and found Lethe sitting on the bank of her river. She dipped a copper bowl into the water, bringing it to her lips and taking a sip.

"Lethe," Hermes called as he approached, "it's so nice to see you."

She rose to her feet and spun around, the hem of her charcoal gray dress swishing at her ankles. "Hello." She cocked her head, her eyes calculating as if she didn't know who he was. "You have a familiar face, but I can't recall your name."

He chuckled. "Perhaps if you didn't drink from the river of forgetfulness, your memory would improve."

She looked at the water before returning her gaze to him. "The river provides me with my power. Without it, I would turn mortal."

"You have to forget in order to do your job?"

She smiled sadly. "It's my lot in life."

"That sucks." But it did give him an idea of what he could offer her in return for her services.

"Indeed." She nodded, her brow furrowing in confusion. "Now, what were we talking about? What is your name again?"

"I'm Hermes."

She tapped her finger against her forehead. "Hermes. Hermes, Hermes, Hermes." She tapped each ear, her nose, and her chin as she repeated his name. "I'll remember now."

He highly doubted it.

"It's nice to meet you in person, Hermes. I have heard so much about you. What can I help you forget? A lover? A friend? If you've lost something, I'm afraid I can't help you find it, but I'm happy to wipe a memory from your mind."

"It isn't I who needs to forget. Can you wipe a memory from the minds of millions?"

She pursed her lips. "All at once?"

He nodded.

Inhaling deeply, she tilted her head. "I don't recall anyone ever asking for such a feat, but that's not saying much. I can't even remember what I had for breakfast."

"I'll talk to Zeus about this for you. See if there's some way you can retain your immortality without having to drink from the river."

"You don't have to do that. This is the life I bargained for; I don't need anything in return."

Hermes blinked, perplexed. "You'll do this for me, and you expect absolutely nothing in return?"

She laughed. "I'm just happy for the company. I rarely get visitors down here."

Interesting. Perhaps Kat was right about this asking for help business. It was certainly easier than the kidnapping scheme he was concocting in his mind.

"I assume you want the memory erased from the mortals above ground?"

"Yes, the living."

She nodded. "I will require safe passage to the surface and the promise of a return trip. I reside here in the underworld, but I don't have a key to get in. Not that I could find my way back to the entrance if I tried. I've never been good at remembering directions."

"Of course. Anything you need."

"How exciting. The last time I stepped foot on the surface was when Hercules needed me to make people forget he lost an arm-wrestling match against Medusa. He was so focused on not looking her in the eyes, he didn't notice her other hand reaching for his crotch. That tale spread quickly amongst the mortals." She laughed and sighed wistfully. "It's been centuries."

"Shall we?" Hermes offered her his arm.

"One moment." She held up a finger and scurried toward the riverbank. "Just let me refuel." Squatting, she dipped her copper bowl into the river and drank the contents before rising to her feet and taking his arm. "Off we go. Whee!" She giggled.

Hermes guided Lethe out of the underworld and through the swamp to his bike. He took his spare helmet from the side pannier and handed it to the goddess.

"What is this machine?" She ran her hand over the seat. "Is it some kind of horseless chariot?"

"Something like that. Put this on your head."

"Why?"

"For protection." Not that he'd ever been in an accident, nor would a god be seriously injured if one happened. But too many states had helmet laws, and it was a pain to keep track of which. So, he always wore his to make things easier.

Lethe put the helmet on and settled on the seat behind him. As she wrapped her arms around him, his mind drifted to the way Kat's body felt pressed against him when they rode. He couldn't wait to take a cross-country trip with her. Or, hell…he'd be happy just riding around town as long as she was with him.

"Where are we going?" Lethe asked as he revved the engine.

"To get my partner in crime." He sped out of the swamp and parked in front of the house on Esplanade.

Kat stood in the doorway as he and Lethe approached, a vision of beauty with her long dark hair cascading around her shoulders, her smile brightening her eyes. "Hi. You must be Lethe. I'm Kat." She held out her hand, and the goddess shook it.

Lethe turned to Hermes. "She's a mortal. Is she important?"

He wrapped an arm around Kat's waist, tugging her to his side. "She's the most important person in my life."

"I see. Tell me your name again."

"It's Kat." Her brow furrowed.

"She has to drink from her own river," he whispered in her ear, and Kat's eyes widened.

"Kat. Kat, Kat, Kat…" Lethe tapped the same spots on her face as she repeated the name. "There. Now I'll remember. Oh, nice house! Can I see the inside? I haven't been above ground in ages." She drifted through the door.

Kat started to follow her, but Hermes caught her hand. "You were right," he said.

"I usually am." She grinned. "Get used to it."

He laughed. "She offered her help with no expectation of repayment, and she didn't judge or ridicule me for needing assistance."

"Some people are cool like that." She kissed his cheek and followed Lethe inside.

The goddess stood in the middle of the living room, her gaze glued to the television, where a local news channel reported on the incident. "According to your magic box, the city is in turmoil." She blinked, confusion contorting her features as she turned to him. "Why am I here again?"

"To make the mortals forget about the turmoil."

"That's right. Yes, yes. I can do that, but…" She pursed her lips. "Kat is an important mortal."

"Very important," he said.

"To perform such widespread magic as you require, I cannot single her out. She will forget too."

Kat gasped and clutched his hand. "I won't remember any of this?"

"Surely there's a way to spare her?" They'd been through so much over the past few days. Would she even remember that she loved him if she lost all the memories?

"What if I speed her away? I can take her to Mexico or Canada and bring her back once the spell is cast."

Lethe shook her head, a sad smile curving her lips. "How far does the magic box reach? Are there others?"

"Everyone has them," Kat said. "They're all over the world."

"Then I'm afraid if you want things to resume as if your incident never happened, the memory wipe will have to be global. It will affect all mortals."

Tears welled in Kat's eyes as she sank onto the couch, and Hermes' heart ached for her. For them.

"Will she have any memories of the past few days?"

"Oh, yes, but it will be like a fog in her mind. She won't be able to recall anything associated with the incident, but everything else will be there."

"Great." Kat leaned back into the cushion. "Everything about the past few days has been related to the caduceus. I won't remember anything."

"I'm sorry, dear." Sympathy filled Lethe's eyes. "I simply don't have the ability to spare you."

"It's fine. I'm as much to blame for all of this as the gods." Kat waved her hand as if waving off her sadness. "I'll give up my memories to fix it."

Hermes sank down next to her, taking her hands in his. "I saw a movie once. I believe it was called *50 First Dates*. The woman lost her memory every night, so they recorded a video for her to watch each morning to remind her."

"I remember it." She let out a sardonic laugh. "I

won't be able to say that about the past few days, will I?"

"Let's make a video. We'll explain everything that happened so you can put the pieces back together."

Kat shrugged. "It's worth a shot."

Hermes showed Lethe how to operate the camera on his phone, and, once she got over her shock and amazement at the "magic" device, she recorded them as they recounted their adventures. As they finished the story, Kat scooted to the edge of the sofa and peered into the camera.

"You're in love with this man, Kat. Please, *please* don't forget that. If you can't remember, just look into his eyes. It's there, somewhere in your heart. Find it."

His own heart ached at her words. "And I'm in love with you." He looked at Kat and then at the camera. "I will work my ass off to prove it to you if you don't remember. Okay?" He nodded at Lethe, and she returned his phone.

"I believe we're ready," he said.

"Hold on." Kat cupped his cheek in her hand, turning his face to hers and planting a passionate kiss on his lips. "I love you, Hermes of Olympus."

"And I love you, my dear, sweet Kathryn, goddess of my heart."

"Aw." Lethe clutched her hands over her chest. "I

wish the Fates would send me a soulmate. It gets lonely down by the river, all by myself."

"Don't give up hope. I've been around for millennia, and I just found mine." He brushed his lips to Kat's before looking at Lethe. "Let's get this over with."

"Great!" She beamed a smile. "What are we doing again?"

Hermes explained what happened. "We need the mortals to forget Pan ever started the so-called sleeping spell, so they'll resume the festivities."

Lethe nodded and sat cross-legged on the floor. "Got it. I'll need silence as I work my magic."

He turned off the television and wrapped his arms around Kat. She leaned into his side, resting her head on his shoulder, and Lethe began her spell.

The energy in the room thickened, gathering around the goddess as she sat silently on the floor. Silver sparkled in her aura, electric, and Kat wrapped her arms tighter around Hermes. The air hummed, thickening even more, creating almost a vacuum as Lethe pulled it toward her. Energy crackled, and in a burst of light and heat, she let it go, shooting it out into the world. She swayed, catching herself with her hands and sinking to the floor.

Kat gasped and straightened. She blinked and

looked at him with questioning eyes. "What just happened? Who is that woman lying on the floor?"

Hermes' stomach sank. He had hoped against hope that his connection with Kat would spare her from the memory loss, but it seemed not even Fate could save her.

"Lethe, are you okay?" he asked.

"I'm fine." She pushed back to a sitting position. "That much magic wipes me out. I need to get back to my river to refuel."

"I'm so confused." Kat brushed the hair from her face and leaned away from him. "How did I get here? Is this your rental house?"

"It is." He sighed. "Lethe wiped your memory. She wiped the memory of all mortals, and I'm so sorry it happened to you. I love you, Kat."

She tilted her head, searching his eyes, her brow furrowing with confusion. "I feel like you've said that to me before, but I can't recall."

He glided his fingers along her cheek. "That's because I have."

Her lips parted on a quick inhale. "I love you too. Why do I feel like I've said it before? I'm sure I haven't."

"You have, dearest." He pulled out his phone and texted her the video they made moments ago. "I have to return Lethe to the underworld. Watch this video, and it will explain everything. Will you be okay here for a few minutes while I'm gone?"

Kat looked at her phone as it pinged. "Yeah. I'll be fine, but won't Zeus be angry that I'm here?"

"The rest of the gods left town. Watch the video, love. I'll be back before you know it."

She narrowed her eyes at him. "I feel like you've told me that before too."

CHAPTER SEVENTEEN

Kat stayed on the couch as Hermes left with the goddess of forgetfulness. Her mind felt like a fog, memories fleeting in but disappearing before she could grasp them.

"What the hell just happened?" She pressed play on the video and saw herself sitting next to Hermes on the couch in this very spot. How long had she been here?

"You stole my caduceus," Hermes said, "and then Pan stole it from you."

She brought her fingers to her lips. Why on earth would she steal from a god…especially the god of thieves? She was smarter than that.

"It's the key to the underworld, so I planned to take it, sneak into Elysium, and apologize to

Camilla."

Oh, okay. That made more sense. She would do anything to relieve the guilt she'd been carrying for the past year. She tried to focus, tried to concentrate on the memory to recall exactly what happened, but it dissolved as she attempted to hold on to it.

She finished the video, and her heart swelled with joy as Hermes professed his love to her. *That* she remembered, though her mind couldn't recall him actually saying the words. She felt it in her soul.

Tucking her phone in her pocket—hold on, whose clothes were these?—she rose to her feet. How she came to be wearing cargo pants and a sweater that didn't belong to her was the least of her concerns at the moment.

"Whew! That's a lot to absorb. I could use some fresh air." She opened the front door and stepped onto the porch. People milled about on the sidewalks, heading toward the French Quarter. Some looked as confused as Kat was, while others smiled and laughed as if nothing had happened. Lethe's magic had worked. Mardi Gras was saved.

Kat returned to her spot on the sofa and watched the video again. She searched her mind for the memories, but the fog dissipated, taking them with it as it left, leaving behind only the emotion.

She knew she loved Hermes, and he loved her. But she would never be able to recall the way it happened.

Sadness sat heavy in her heart, but as the door swung open and Hermes stepped through, she smiled in spite of it. "That was fast."

"I am the god of speed." In the blink of an eye, she found him sitting on the sofa next to her.

"That much I remember." She leaned toward him and kissed him.

"I will do whatever it takes to rebuild your love for me." He trailed the backs of his fingers down her cheek.

"There's nothing to rebuild. The feeling is still there; I just can't recall where it came from."

He lifted the locket in his fingers, opening it and gazing at the photos inside. "I promised I'd deliver this to your sister. I intend to keep it."

A tear slid down her cheek, and he wiped it away with his thumb. "I wish I could see her one more time. I wish I could apologize in person."

He closed the locket and let it rest against her chest. "I can't take a mortal into the underworld."

"I know. I remember you saying that when we first met."

Hermes looked at her, his eyes filling with

emotion as he inhaled a deep breath. "I can't take a mortal, but I could take a goddess."

She laughed dryly. "That doesn't help me much, does it?" She unclasped the necklace and placed it in his palm. "Please tell her I'm sorry and that I love her."

He closed his hand around the locket and lowered it into his lap before letting out a heavy sigh. "It seems the god of language is having a hard time communicating for the first time in his existence."

He grasped her hand, lacing his fingers through hers. "You make me a better man, Kat. And I want to spend the rest of my life with you, no matter how long that life may be."

She looked at their entwined fingers before gazing into his eyes. "What are you saying?"

He swallowed hard. "I'm immortal, and you are not."

"Thanks for pointing out the obvious." Surely he wasn't suggesting that he…

"We have two options here. I can take this to your sister and deliver your message. When I return, I will give up my immortality to stay with you here in New Orleans."

Kat gaped. "What? Are you crazy? You're Hermes, god of speed, of travel, of thieves, and nearly every other gods-damned thing. What would the world do without you?"

"The world doesn't need me anymore, but I need you." He scooted closer until his knee touched hers. "You taught me that, Kat. That it's okay to need someone. I can't live without you."

"No, Hermes. I won't let you do that. I've got fifty years of my life left. You've existed for millennia, and you will for millennia more."

"I would rather spend the next fifty years with you by my side than live the rest of eternity without you."

She shook her head. As much as she loved this man, she could not be the reason a god died. It wasn't right. "What's the other option? You said there were two."

He placed the locket in her hand. "You could take this to your sister yourself, and then spend the rest of eternity with me."

"What do you mean?"

"I can make you immortal. You could be a goddess and spend forever with me… If you think you can put up with me for that long."

"How? I thought the only way a mortal could become immortal was if they consumed ambrosia. You said all the fields were razed."

He chuckled, shaking his head. "Have you forgotten who you're dealing with?"

She raised her brows. "The god of thieves... Did you...?"

He pulled a small glass jar from his pocket and held it toward her. "Of course I took some before it was all gone. I was saving it for a special occasion, and I can't think of a single moment that would be better than you saying yes."

She took the jar, peering at the thick amber liquid inside. Immortality and an eternity with Hermes? "Where would we live?"

"Home base has to be Seattle. Zeus's orders. But with you as a goddess, I won't have to hold back on the speed when we travel. We can go anywhere, anytime."

"We can come back to New Orleans to visit my friends?"

"As often as you like."

This was crazy. Was she really considering this? "What about my job? My sister's medical bills..."

"Dearest, when you've been around as long as I have, you amass a small..." he laughed, "a not-so-small fortune. Your debts will be paid; you'll never suffer injury or illness, and you'll live forever."

"And I can worship your body every night?"

"Only after I'm done worshipping yours. What do you say? Will you spend forever with me?"

She sucked in a shaky breath, her stomach fluttering as she looked into his eyes. "I would love to."

Cupping her hand in his, he twisted the lid from the jar. "You'll need to drink it all. It's thick like honey, but it goes down smooth."

Holy Hades. She was about to drink the nectar of the gods…and become a fucking goddess herself. She blinked, pinching herself hard on her arm, and she winced.

"Are you okay?"

"Just making sure I'm not dreaming. I don't know what I did to win your heart, but I'm so happy that it's mine." She tipped back the jar and poured the ambrosia into her mouth.

The thick liquid was sweet, first tasting of exotic fruits and then smoothing into a warm honey-like flavor. As she swallowed, it coated her throat, both cooling and warming her insides, all the way to her core.

Hermes stroked her hand, adoration filling his eyes and an elated smile lighting on his lips. "How do you feel, dearest?"

"I feel…" Her vision tunneled, darkness closing in around her as a sinking sensation pulled her under.

She lost consciousness for a moment—at least, it felt like only a moment—before a burst of sparkling silver light brought her back to the present. Coolness flushed through her veins, erasing every ache and itch from her body.

She felt light, calm, complete. "I feel wonderful. Oh!" She clutched her head as the memories of the past few days tumbled through her mind: taking the staff, being knocked out by Pan, making love to Hermes… "I remember now. I remember it all."

He pulled her into his arms and kissed her. "You just made all my dreams come true."

She laughed. "You made me a goddess."

"I did indeed."

She gasped. "My calico. Can I still shift?" That was a question she should have asked *before* she drank the ambrosia. *Good going, Kat.*

"Try and see." Hermes released her, and she rose to her feet.

Nausea churned in her stomach. If she'd lost her calico, she didn't know what she'd do. Her feline was as much a part of her as her ass was. With a deep inhale, she called on her magic, drawing her calico from its slumber in her soul.

In an instant, her paws hit the floor, and she

froze, waiting for the awful skin-crawling sensation to paralyze her. It didn't happen.

She leaped onto the sofa and shifted back to her human form, again with no pain whatsoever. She laughed. "It doesn't hurt anymore."

"It never will again." He hooked the locket around her neck. "Are you ready to see your sister now?"

"Hell yeah, I am."

As they left the house and climbed onto Hermes' bike, parade music drifted on the air. New Orleans had returned to normal, but Kat's normal had taken on a whole new meaning. She wrapped her arms around her god—*her* god…would she ever get used to that?—and he pulled out onto the road.

He wasn't kidding when he said he wouldn't hold back on the speed. The entire world blurred as he sped to the swamp. She blinked maybe three times before they arrived at the forest edge. She expected to be dizzy as all get-out when she slid off the seat, but the ride hadn't affected her equilibrium in the slightest. "That was exhilarating."

He smiled. "I'm glad you enjoyed it. Hop on." He turned his back to her, and she jumped on with ease before he dashed past the bokor's place and deposited her in the boat.

Her pulse thrummed as they crossed the swamp and docked by the underworld entrance. Her stomach soured like she'd drunk expired buttermilk, and when Hermes tapped his staff against the door, unlocking it, her legs trembled.

She was immortal now, but entering the realm of the dead scared the shit out of her. How on earth did she think she could do this as a mortal?

She clutched Hermes' hand in a death grip—pun intended—and followed him down a rocky trail to an obsidian river. A tall, creepy-looking dude in black robes paddled a boat toward them and gestured for them to get in.

"Three times in one day?" His voice was gravelly like he didn't use it much. "I'll have to start charging you double."

Hermes laughed and placed two silver coins in his skeletal hand. "Charon, I'd like you to meet Kathryn, goddess of…" He paused, rubbing his thumb and forefinger on his beard. "Goddess of cats and redemption."

"Redemption?" She took his hand and stepped into the boat.

"You turned your life around, and you've made me a better man. It's fitting."

As they reached the other side of the river, she

followed him across a field, and sure enough, there in front of her lay an actual yellow brick road. "I feel like we should skip down it, but I'm too anxious. Can you take me there quickly?"

He swept her into his arms. "Quick is my middle name."

Kat blinked again, and they stood at the edge of Elysium. Rolling fields with colorful flowers expanded in front of her, and spirits milled about, all smiling, all peaceful. As she stepped onto the grass, the rocky walls of the cavernous underworld dissolved away and blue sky stretched above her head as far as she could see. "Is this really part of the underworld?"

Hermes stepped beside her, wrapping an arm around her waist. "It is, dearest. The sky and breeze are an illusion made to reward those who led good lives."

"How do I find my sister?"

"Simply call her name."

She inhaled deeply, letting out a slow breath before inhaling again. "Camilla." Her voice came out as a whisper, but a whisper was all she needed. Her sister manifested before her.

"Kat? Oh my gods. What are you doing here? What happened? How did you die?" Camilla threw her arms around Kat's shoulders and hugged her tight. She felt solid and warm, like she did when she was living, but her skin held a rosy glow, and her eyes were bright with life.

A sob bubbled up from deep inside her as she closed her eyes, memorizing the way Camilla felt in her arms. "I'm so sorry."

Her sister pulled away and rested her hands on her shoulders. "You have nothing to be sorry for. Tell me how you got here."

"Hermes brought me." She reached for his hand, and he moved toward her.

"Wow! You must have done something really amazing before you died to be escorted here by Hermes himself."

"I'm not dead." She slid her arm around his waist. "I am his goddess." Man, oh, man, did that sound weird. Kat Gataki, a goddess. Who'd have thought?

Camilla's eyes widened with wonder, her mouth forming the shape of an O as she gaped. "Holy cow. Mom has to hear this."

Kat's chest ached. "She's here too?"

"Of course she is. Hey, Mom, Kat's here, and she's a goddess!" Camilla called, and her mother materialized by her side.

"Mom." Kat covered her mouth and sobbed again.

"Hello, my darling." She pulled her into a hug. "Immortality looks good on you. How did this come to be?"

Kat told them the story of meeting Hermes and Pan's shenanigans that ultimately led to them falling in love.

"The Fates had a hand in it," Hermes added. "So I promise you this was meant to be, and I will worship your daughter like the goddess she is for the rest of eternity."

"Damn right you will." Her mom winked.

Kat turned to her sister and unclasped the locket before placing it in her hand. "I came here to apologize to you." A tear slid down her cheek. "I was selfish and cruel, and I should never have said those things to you. I should have gotten this from the car, and I'm so sorry that you had to come here without it. Can you ever forgive me?"

"Forgive you?" Camilla shook her head. "You took care of me until I died. You sacrificed your life to help me with mine. You've done absolutely nothing that requires forgiveness. I love you, Sis. I've never held that night against you."

Kat's chest warmed, the heavy weight she'd been carrying in her heart lifting as she looked into her sister's eyes. "You have no idea how much this means to me. I have felt so guilty."

"Don't. Everything is as it should be." She pressed the locket into Kat's palm. "Keep it as a reminder that you are loved, and you always will be."

"We miss you," her mom said, "but we are so happy that you have found joy."

"I'll come back and visit." She looked at Hermes for confirmation, and he nodded.

"Of course, dearest. We can come back anytime."

She hugged her family and said her goodbyes before Hermes returned her to the surface. They walked hand in hand at a mortal's pace past the bokor's house. The old troll stepped onto the porch, but when he saw their faces, he quickly bowed his head and returned inside.

Kat grinned. This goddess business would take some getting used to.

They arrived at Hermes' bike, and he handed her a helmet. "How are you feeling?"

"Like the world has finally lifted from my shoulders and I can breathe. Thank you for that, Hermes. Thank you for everything."

"The pleasure has been mine. I love you."

She stepped into his arms and kissed him. "And I love you, god of thieves."

"I certainly wasn't ready for the one who stole my heart, but I am so happy you did."

"So… What's next?"

Hermes grinned slyly. "We have the house for another week. How about we have a little pre-honeymoon before we head to Seattle and say our vows?"

"I like the way you think, mister." She trailed a finger down his stomach, stopping just above the waistband of his jeans. "Can I drive?"

He glanced at his bike before arching a brow at her. "Anything for you, dearest."

Fire Witches of Salem Series

Chaos and Ash

Commanding Chaos

Claiming Chaos

Mayhem and Ember

Mending Mayhem

Mastering Mayhem

Discord and Cinder

Demanding Discord

Desiring Discord

Collection One: Books 1-3

Collection Two: Books 4-6

Collection Three: Books 7-9

New Orleans Nocturnes Series

License to Bite

Shift Happens

Life's a Witch

Santa Got Run Over by a Vampire

Finders Reapers

Swipe Right to Bite

Batshift Crazy

Holy Shift

Collection One: Books 1-3

Collection Two: Books 4-7

Crescent City Wolf Pack Series

Werewolves Only

Beneath a Blue Moon

Bound by Blood

A Deal with Death

A Song to Remember

Shifting Fate

Collection One: Books 1-3

Collection Two: Books 4-6

Haunted Ever After Series

Love at First Haunt

Second Chance Spirit

Third Time's a Ghost

Love and Ghosts

Love and Omens

Love and Curses

Collection One: Books 1 - 3

Collection Two: Books 4 - 6

Lessons in Divine Disasters Series

How to Steal a God's Heart

How to Flirt With the Angel of Death

How to Woo the World's First Vampire

Stand Alone Books

Flipping the Bird

The Rest of Forever

Soul Catchers

Bewitching the Vampire

Carrie Pulkinen is a paranormal romance author who has always been fascinated with things that go bump in the night. Of course, when you grow up next door to a cemetery, the dead (and the undead) are hard to ignore. Pair that with her passion for writing and her love of a good happily-ever-after, and becoming a paranormal romance author seems like the only logical career choice.

Before she decided to turn her love of the written word into a career, Carrie spent the first part of her professional life as a high school journalism and yearbook teacher. She loves good chocolate and bad puns, and in her free time, she likes to dance, drink wine, and travel with her family.

Connect with Carrie online:
CarriePulkinen.com